Archibald Sinclair, Dùghall Bochannan

Reminiscences of the Life and Labours of Dugald Buchanan

formerly teacher and evangelist at Rannoch, Perthshire - with his Spiritual songs

and an English version of them

Archibald Sinclair, Dùghall Bochannan

Reminiscences of the Life and Labours of Dugald Buchanan
formerly teacher and evangelist at Rannoch, Perthshire - with his Spiritual songs and an English version of them

ISBN/EAN: 9783337262389

Printed in Europe, USA, Canada, Australia, Japan

Cover: Foto ©Andreas Hilbeck / pixelio.de

More available books at **www.hansebooks.com**

REMINISCENCES.

—o—

CHAPTER I.

" Train up a child in the way he should go ; and when he is old,
he will not depart from it."—Prov. xxii. 6.

Highland Literature and Poets—Macdonald—M'Intyre—Ross—Buchanan
—Buchanan's Birth and Parentage—Parental Solicitude regarding
him—Early Religious Impressions—His Mother's death—Early
Visions of Death and Judgment—Alarm—Anxiety on Cessation of
these Dreams—Depression—Reflections—Samuel Rutherford.

TILL within a period comparatively recent, printed
literature was scarce in the Highlands of Scotland.
Of oral literature—as tales, legends, historical tra-
ditions, and the compositions of the bards, there was
no lack. Poetry was in great demand, and good
poets held in corresponding estimation. Their choice
productions were carefully stored in memory—
recited at festivals, and bridal gatherings ; and during
the long winter evenings, whiled away many a long
hour. Thus, by the combined powers of memory and
oral recitation, such compositions were preserved even
among an uneducated people ; and transmitted with
accuracy that does credit to their powers of memory.
For example, we have in the " Book of the Dean of
Lismore," a piece of poetry from the recitation of a
Caithness female, word for word almost, as it was

A

transcribed by the Dean centuries before. Thus we see, how poetry such as Dugald Buchanan's, obtained wide circulation, even among an illiterate people ; and became a power on the side of evangelical truth. His wit, his merit, his superiority, were universally allowed. Even those who cared not for the religious element of his poems, were captivated by the charm of the poetry ; and thus, multitudes became familiar with gospel truths that would never otherwise have known them. Buchanan is the first of our high-class Highland poets, who dedicated his gifts to the service of religion. His bardic fellow-countrymen—Macdonald, M'Intyre, Ross, and others, tuned their lyres to worldly themes—more popular by far with the masses, than the higher themes of Buchanan's muse. It is no little evidence therefore of his power, that while only a few editions of their works, of acknowledged literary merit, have been printed, Dugald Buchanan's spiritual songs have been published twenty times, and with undiminished popularity and favour.

Balquidder, the country of the freebooter Rob Roy M'Gregor, gave birth to Dugald Buchanan. In those days railways were unknown ; even roads were few and far between. Now the railway train, which speeds daily along those once inaccessible regions, brings them within easy reach of any holiday sight-seeker, who has time and inclination to enjoy wild Highland scenery. The tourist, as he finds his way south, has marked the stream that issues from Loch-voil, and winds its sluggish course along the valley of Strathyre, in the direction of Lochlubnaig. It is the Balvaig—a name descriptive of its silent, stealthy flow. Shortly before the train arrives at Strathyre station, there may be seen, standing on the other side of this stream, a farm-house. This is the farm of Ardoch, where Dugald Buchanan was born. His father rented the farm, and was owner of a small meal mill there—the remains of which are still standing. Our author was born sometime in the year 1716, a year after Rob Roy had marshalled his men on the field of Sheriffmuir, under the banner of the Pretender.

Both his parents were estimable persons, people of sterling Christian worth—of that class which constitutes the very bone and sinew of a healthy commonwealth. He speaks of his mother with great veneration and affection. " I had the blessing to be born of religious parents, who took great care to train me in the fear of the Lord ; especially my tender mother, who taught me to pray as soon as I could speak, following all the means used for my improvement, with her fervent prayers at a throne of grace for my conversion." With the Psalmist, he could say, " I am thy servant, the son of thy handmaid." She was his mother, according to the flesh, and his mother in the Lord. To her early instruction, we trace those impressions never erased. Rarely, says a divine of a bygone age, do the faithful instructions of a child, especially by a pious mother, fail to bear fruit. And to Buchanan's early training we may safely ascribe the beginnings of that Christianity for which, in after years, he was so distinguished. That he was at a very early period the subject of religious impressions, the following passage from his diary shows. " To the best of my recollection, when between five and six years of age, I went on a Sabbath day, without my mother's knowledge, and amused myself foolishly ; and though I returned before my absence was observed, yet my mind was filled with heavy accusations of conscience for breaking the Sabbath. Previously I did not pray unless pressed to it by my mother ; but now I began to pray without any entreaty."

In 1722 his excellent mother died. Of the loss he thus sustained, he speaks with deep emotion. Her example, her instruction, her maternal solicitude for his soul's welfare, were, he says, "as the thorns that hedged up my way, on the removal of which I began to slight duty. Like Joash, I did well all the days of Jehoiada ; but when Jehoiada died, I discovered myself to be what I really was." Once and again these early impressions, both in his own judgment, and that of others, seemed entirely erased. But we find they were at certain intervals revived— each revival constituting a link in the chain of successive convictions, by which eventually he was led to find permanent repose upon the bosom of his beloved Saviour. One of these intermittent awakenings is as follows—all the more remarkable, when we consider the tender age at which such thoughts passed through his mind. The readers of his " Day of Judgment " will recognise one of the germs of that imagery, which has made that poem so grand and impressive. " The Lord began to visit me with terrible visions, which greatly frightened me. I always dreamed that the day of judgment was come; that Christ appeared to judge the world, that all people were gathered before His throne; and that He separated them into companies. I found myself along with others, sentenced to everlasting burnings; always saw myself entering into the flames, and would instantly awake with fear and trembling." For two years in succession, these visions came at intervals; always with deeply solemnising effect, and were regarded by him as divine monitions sent to warn him. "God," says he, "speaketh once, yea, twice, yet man perceiveth it not. In a dream, in a vision of the night, when deep sleep falleth upon man, in slumbering upon his bed. Then he openeth the ear of men, and sealeth instructions, that he may draw man from his purpose, and hide pride from man." (Job xxxiii. 14-17.) When these dreams ceased, he was equally alarmed. His alarm was greatly intensified, as his eye incidentally caught the following scripture (Gen. vi. 3):—"My spirit shall not always strive with man." "These visions," says he to himself, "are the Spirit's strivings with me; and now that they, have ceased, I fear that the strivings of the Divine Spirit with me have ceased also. I have quenched Him." Gloomy thoughts took possession of him. He concluded that his salvation was hopeless. He thought of God only as an angry God, and discontinued former religious duties, regarding them as useless formalities, and lived, as he tells us, from his ninth till his twelfth year, in a kind of stupid despair, often thinking of the words, "My Spirit shall not always strive with man."

He closes the portion of his diary that ends with his twelfth year with the following observations:—

" When I reflect upon this early period of my life, and consider the natural inclinations of my mind, my belief is more firmly established in the truth of the doctrine, that I am just what the Pharisees said of the blind man whom Christ restored to sight, ' altogether born in sin.'   " Foolishness is bound up in the heart of a child ;" and although the rod of correction, while held over him, may drive it far away from him, it can never drive it so far as to prevent its turning again, till the sanctifying grace of Christ is exerted. Besides the clear scriptural proof of original sin, experience puts it beyond doubt with myself, that I came to the world with the seeds of all manner of sin sown in my heart.   Instead of honouring God with my first fruits, Satan got the first fruits of all my labours.   I did no duty to which I was not pressed by my parents, or by a slavish fear of hell.   He who knows God aright, will be influenced by motives different from these.   The love of God will be his main principle.   The sweetness and delight enjoyed in his service will be sufficient to induce any one to serve him.

" When I reflect on the disposition of my heart at this early period, I find that I am full of pride and covetousness, hatred, and revenge, which manifest themselves on the slightest occasion.   Whence did these come ?   Who taught them to me ?   I find they were not imbibed from others.   Before I had access to those by whom my morals could be contaminated I found these corrupt inclinations in my nature.   They proceeded solely from myself. 'As a fountain casteth out her waters, so she casteth out her wickedness.' When I take a retrospective view of this period of my life, I am led to see the absolute necessity of regeneration by grace, for renewing our nature, and restoring the lost image of God in the soul. Man is helpless and hopeless in himself."

Such are Buchanan's reflections on the years of his childhood—those years of comparatively little guilt—the period of man's natural life when he makes the nearest approximation to innocence. Yet how far from righteousness are we even then ! And how true as well as touching, are the words of Samuel Rutherford:—"I have nothing but my loathsomeness to commend me to Christ. He must take me as I am, for nothing, or not take me at all."

CHAPTER II.

DUGALD BUCHANAN received the rudiments of education in one of the schools belonging to the Society for Promoting Christian Knowledge—a society that has done good work as pioneer of similar societies, and as an active agent in the Lord's vineyard. It was founded by a few devoted Christian gentlemen in Edinburgh, who, in the year 1701, formed themselves into "a society for the reformation of manners." In 1709, it received the patronage of Queen Anne, and was erected into a corporation. As described in that patent, its object is "the promotion of Christian knowledge, the increase of piety and virtue within Scotland, especially in the Highlands, Islands, and remote corners thereof, where error, idolatry, superstition, and ignorance do mostly abound, because of the largeness of the parishes, and the scarcity of schools." In 1800 its schools numbered 300, and upwards of 30,000 persons had received religious instruction.

One of these schools was planted in Buchanan's native parish, under the charge of Mr Nicol Ferguson. He makes no mention of him in his diary; but from the care with which the society chose its teachers, Ferguson, we believe, was a man of Christian character, as well as fair literary acquirements. How long Buchanan was in this school we know not; nor what progress he made. But at the age of twelve years he was considered qualified for the situation of tutor, which anyhow shows that he made fair progress for one so young. But this early initiation into what was to be his future life-work was not a happy one. He speaks in melancholy terms of the family with which he thus became associated. "They were remarkable," he says, "for every kind of profanity, with the exception of the mistress of the household," who was an excellent person. The result of mingling with such associates might be anticipated, in the case of one of his tender age, and without settled religious convictions. "I was," he says, "scarcely a month in this family when I learned to speak the language of Ashdod. In a short time I exceeded every one of them. I could not speak without uttering oaths and imprecations. I sinned without restraint—except when I thought of death. Then I became dejected and sad; concluding I was undone, and that to refrain from sin was unavailing." His terrors of mind were at times overwhelming. His only relief was, that death was at a distance, and should he eventually perish, meantime he had nothing to fear. But he was not permitted to solace himself with these vain imaginations. Now and again something happened that dispelled such fancies, and in which providences he saw, in years of greater light, the hand of the Lord, for the eventual fulfilment of his purposes of love and mercy towards him. He narrates several such incidents. For example, on a Sabbath evening the mistress of the family read the Scriptures to the household, and spoke solemnly of eternity and judgment. She described the manner of the judgment, and the second coming of the Lord. She said it was the opinion of some that it would take place on a Sabbath, and in the winter season—and that his appearance would be heralded by thunder, lightning, and hail. That same night there was a violent storm, such as she described. Hail poured into the room in which he slept; and its walls were illuminated with vivid flashes of lightning. He trembled with apprehension; believing that at any moment Jesus might appear, and summon the dead to rise. " O, how happy would I be if I could be buried under the ruins of the house, and hide from the face of the Judge. Horror seized upon me. Repentance, I thought, was too late. I remembered one of Mr Gray's sermons, in which he describes the torments of the damned, and their consternation at the coming of the Lord. I thought if my life were to begin again, how I should read, and pray, and keep the Sabbath. I heartily resolved against my sins, but my resolutions were soon at an end. In less than eight days I was just what I was before."

Other incidents, as the following, dispelled the fond hope, that as he was young, the day was at a distance when the grim messenger would come to summon him. " I remember being in a boat on a large loch.

In consequence of a storm, we were in danger of
being drowned. But the Lord, who is kind to the
unthankful, brought us safe to land, after we had
despaired of our lives." This happened while resident
in the forementioned family, in which he was tutor.
The following happened after his return to Ardoch.
He bathed in the Balvaig, and, going too near the
brink, the sand gave way. He sank, and would have
been drowned, but that the current floated him so near
the bank of the river, as to enable a little girl, who
watched his fate, to bring him to shore by a hay rake.
These incidents deeply impressed him. At the age of
fourteen years he went to Stirling, probably to prose-
cute his education. Allusions in his diary lead to the
inference that he early showed a precocity of intellec-
tual vigour, that promised future eminence; and
which encouraged friends to make special efforts to
promote his educational efficiency. He remained at
Stirling for the space of two years, and very much in
his former condition of alternate deadness and alarm—the
latter, upon the whole, preponderating, and deepened at
times by incidents similar to those we have narrated.
For example, while here, he fell sick of fever, and
death stared him in the face. "All my old sins came
fresh to me. My bodily trouble was nothing to the
agony of my mind. I earnestly prayed to the Lord
to spare me, that I might have space to repent. I
bound myself under the most solemn vows to serve
the Lord. He heard me, and I was brought again
from the gates of death. But he adds in his own
quaint way—and to show how vain resolutions are
unless God makes his grace sufficient for us—"I was

scarcely recovered from my sickness, when I fell sick of my vows." Another circumstance that made a deep impression, was an escape from the bayonet of a drunken soldier. As the soldier staggered along the street, children amused themselves by throwing dirty rags at him. Buchanan took one of them to throw it away, and the soldier, supposing he meant to join in the frolic, pursued him, and would have stabbed him to death, but that he stumbled in the act of doing it, and so gave time to escape. Not long subsequent to this incident, he had a narrow escape from drowning in the river Carron. Heavy rains fell during that day, and as it was dark before he came to the ford, he did not see that the stream had swollen. His horse was nearly carried off his feet by the force of the current, and he saved himself only by a timely retreat, which he effected with difficulty and danger. At the next stage of his journey he heard that a traveller had been drowned that very evening when attempting to cross by that same ford. These, and similar incidents, he records in his diary, not on account of anything very unusual in the incidents themselves, as because of their bearing upon his religious life. He was a great observer of how providences—" God's most holy, wise, and powerful, preserving, and governing of all his creatures, with all their actions "—were made subservient to the economy of redemption. And as the normal condition of his mind was one of deadness and apathy to spiritual things, he remarks how these occurrences had for a time an awakening and solemnising effect in a very marked manner, though, as he tells us, he had not yet felt the power of the great reforming motive, the love of Christ. Yet, side by side with this habitual tendency to relapse, so characteristic of this period of his life, we find a latent sensibility of conscience, which could be touched by the slightest circumstance, and awakened into intense activity. This shows that, underlying all his superincumbent hopelessness and spiritual apathy, there were seeds of divine grace, which, by God's blessing, time developed into Christian fruitfulness. For example, he was at Edinburgh, in company, when the conversation turned upon religious subjects. One of the party, seeing Buchanan in the Highland costume, and attracted by the vivacity of his conversation—very likely not then of a serious sort—asked him what his religious principles were? He replied somewhat jauntily, that as yet he was like a sheet of white paper, and that he might write any principles he pleased upon him. "Are you indeed?" the stranger replied, "if so, I will give you an advice; take good care that the devil does not scrawl something upon you, and then you will no more be clean." "I was confounded," he says, "by this answer. I did not know which way to look, for it pierced me to the heart to think of the truth of what he said, and which, indeed, the devil had already done. I was also ashamed that I had spoken so irreverently of religion, and firmly resolved never to speak in such a manner again. When I came away, this man's words cleaved very close to me, nor could I by any means get them out of my mind. They also continually brought my former despairing thoughts fresh upon me, and how the devil had written his own law on my heart, and put his image on all my actions."

After being six months in Edinburgh, he returned home to Ardoch. He was now in his eighteenth year, and his father was anxious he should enter upon some profession or trade for his future maintenance in life. To this proposal, however, he did not heartily respond ; on the contrary, he was averse to the restraints and application necessarily involved in the duties of a regular profession. " I loved my loose way of living so well, that I could not think of any other." His friends, however, prevailed upon him to accede to his father's request, and he was apprenticed for three years to a house carpenter in the parish of Kippen—a step in many respects conducive to his good. He associated with a better class of companions. He attended with greater regularity at the house of God—which in years bygone he seldom saw ; and he also profited by the ministrations of Mr Potter, minister of that parish. He mentions specially a series of sermons he preached on Job xxii. 21 : " Acquaint thyself with him and be at peace, and thereby good shall come into thee." He saw, contrary to the gloomy views he formerly held, that salvation, even his salvation, was not impossible. For the time, a ray of hope dawned upon him ; the Lord, he thought, may have mercy even for me, and feeble as the hope was, it had effect upon him. " I abandoned my former careless ways. I had brokenness of heart for sin, and found sweetness in this promise, ' I, even I am he that blotteth out thy transgressions for mine own sake, and will not remember thy sins,' Isa. xliii. 25. But, he adds, " I did not rightly or evangelically understand the true meaning, especially of the words, ' for mine own name's sake.' My legal heart meant another thing, even my prayers, tears, and other acts of duty." Although, therefore, he was for a time relieved from the gloom that formerly settled upon him—because his salvation, as he thought, was hopeless—he fell again into the same despairing state of mind, " because he sought it, not by faith, but as it were by the works of the law." * The law cannot heal a wounded conscience, and as yet he had not attained to Him " whom God hath set forth to be a propitiation through faith in His blood." Therefore he struggled along, and strove, in his own way, to be eased of his burden. " I entered into a covenant with God against sin. I bound myself with the penalty of eternal damnation, in the event of my breaking it. But such was the power of sin in me, that should hell itself appear in all its terrors before me, I would break. through the hedge." Once and again he renewed these vows, limiting them to a shorter period of time, in hopes he would thus succeed better in stemming the tide of his corruptions. But all these self-imposed restraints were swept away as by a mighty torrent ; and he lay in the dust, prostrate before his foe, " that was mightier than he." His experience at this period of life, he gives as follows :—" I looked to some good I

---

* " Go to God with this—' Lord save me, for Christ died for the ungodly ; ' and I am of them. Fling yourself right on to this, as a man commits himself right to the lifebelt amid the surging billows. ' But I do not feel,' says one. Trust not your feelings even if you do feel ; but with no feelings and no hopes of your own, cling desperately to this, ' Christ died for the ungodly.' As ungodly rest you on'this, ' Christ died for the ungodly.' Accept this truth, and you are saved."—*Spurgeon*.

had done, or expected to do in time to come.* Then in my despair I took my fill of sinful enjoyments, while I might have them. I indulged in the dissipation of idle and worldly companionship ; and when in private, I diverted myself by repeating all the songs and ballads I could get." Finding any or all of these utterly unavailing to give rest to his troubled spirit, as a last resource, he tried to persuade himself there was no God ; and that the doctrine of a future judgment and endless punishment, was an idle imagination. In these views he was encouraged by a companion who professed to support his statements by arguments drawn from the divine goodness. Buchanan in his then unhappy condition of mind, gladly received these false views. " I thought," says he, " there was hope for me, since hell was not eternal, but only for a time. O sweet doctrine to such as I was, who looked for nothing but everlasting punishment. I might now indulge in hope, that sometime my torment might come to an end." But the relief he had from these delusions was but temporary. The fire was only smothered, not extinguished. By and by it burned afresh. No ingenious sophistry, no effort of self-righteous activity, no zeal, could assuage the terrors that assailed him. " I saw that in a short time I would go to my place. I had continually a vehement thirst, and drank a great

---

* "This is frequently the case with an awakened soul without clear views of the way of salvation. He is looking to himself instead of looking to Christ for deliverance. He is like the Israelite bitten by a fiery serpent who applies the remedies of men to his wound. They are of no avail. He must look to the brazen serpent or die. Even so the poor sinner must look to Christ or die. ' Believe in the Lord Jesus Christ, and thou shalt be saved.'"—*Anon.*

quantity of water.   When I got a drink I would say,
'Oh ! poor wretch that you are, you will ere long be
with Dives in the flames of hell, where you will not
get as much as a drop of water to cool your scorching
tongue.'   I stood confounded, yea astonished to think
of eternity.   Oh ! how gladly would I be a dog or
any other animal than a man.   In that case death
would put an end to all my miseries.   But now all my
sorrows, which know no end, were but beginning."
Such is the account he gives of the state of mind he
was now in—enduring terrible alarms of conscience—
then relapsing into spiritual deadness, struggling
against his corruptions, and then giving full swing to
his ungodliness—at one time hoping, at another time
despairing, almost to distraction of mind—attending
religious ordinances, and abandoning them.   Not
able to embrace the promises of the Gospel, he un-
sparingly applied to himself the denunciatory doctrines
of the Bible.   This made the house of God a terror to
him ; and for a season he ceased to go to it.   In his
own words, his condition of mind at this period, "was
one of stupid despair—on the whole believing that for
him it was hopeless to expect salvation."   He was
now in the twenty-fourth year of his age, had left
Kippen, and had entered upon a new engagement
with another master in the town of Dumbarton.

CHAPTER III.

" I will bring the blind by a way that they knew not ; I will
lead them in paths that they have not known : I will make darkness light before them, and crooked things straight.   These things
will I do unto them, and not forsake them."—Isa. XLII. 16.

Conversation with his Sister—Reformation—Persecution—Worldly Coun-
sel—Fiery Temptations—Deliverance—Imperfect Views of the Gospel
—Effort to lay hold on Christ—Conversation with a Christian Woman
—Muthil—Cambuslang—Comrie—Treatise on Justification—Kilsyth
—Joy—Spiritual Pride—Depression—Deliverance—His Charter for
the Heavenly Inheritance—Old Scenes—Contrast—Fasting and Con-
fession—Laying hold on Christ—Enlargement—Port of Monteith—
—Kilsyth—Mr Robe—Trouble and Deliverance—Spirit of Revenge—
Desertion of Soul for Two Years—Muthil—Recovery—Resignation to
the Divine Will.

THE first solid relief he had from this melancholy
state of mind was through a pious sister—and in the
twenty-fifth year of his age.   Although he did not all
at once get settled peace in believing, yet this interview gave an impulse in the right direction, which
eventually led to emancipation from his long continued bondage.   Accordingly, for the first time, we
find him giving a date in his diary, which shows the
importance he attached to this event in his spiritual
history.

10th June 1741.—" This is the month in which
the wild ass was found "—in allusion to Jer. ii. 24 ;
and as expressive also of the result of the above interview.   It was the evening of the Lord's day.   He
was carelessly wandering in the fields, as was his

wont ; for he had ceased to attend upon the public ordinances of grace. His sister met him ; gently remonstrated with him for profaning the Sabbath, and for abandoning the house of God. " What do you think will become of you ?" she said. " If you die in your present condition, you will certainly perish." At first he made light of her words ; but she insisted and warned him, that unless he repented he would inevitably perish. His reply was, " You need not tell me so, I am fully aware of it." , " Strange," she replied. " Do you know that you will perish ; are you in despair of mind, or what ? " On ascertaining the condition he was in, she entreated him to look to the blood of Jesus Christ, which cleanseth from sins even of crimson dye. He replied, " That he had counted that blood as an unholy thing ; and had done despite to the Spirit of grace." Thereupon she inquired if he ever prayed, and when he had last done so ? " I have not bowed my knee to God for four years," was the answer. She then besought him to go to a throne of grace that very night. To this he replied, " I will never pray," which he had fully resolved not to do ; for he had utterly despaired of salvation ; and therefore looked upon the ordinances of grace as useless formalities in his case. At this period, he could not presume as much as to mention the name of God ; believing that doing so aggravated his condemnation. His sister, however, who dearly loved him, and longed for his salvation, earnestly urged him to pray and humble himself before God, " who," she said, " would have mercy upon him, as a poor condemned sinner, and grant him salva-

tion." * Her earnest and loving solicitations, by the
blessing of God, prevailed, and he prostrated himself at
a throne of mercy. " I stood," he says, " like the
publican afar off, and said, God be merciful to me
a sinner—not out of compliment as before, but
from a real sense of guilt and misery. I did
not expect to be heard. Satan and my unbelief
said, I was a great fool to expect the Lord
would show mercy to the like of me."† But the God
who hears prayer, not for our sake, but " for his name's
sake," heard Dugald Buchanan ; and the result he
tells us in the following words. " The Lord instructed
me with a secret and powerful conviction that my
sins were pardonable, notwithstanding their heinous
aggravations, and that His name would be glorified
in pardoning even the like of me." The relief he felt
was great, and showed itself in his external deport-
ment. The change was observed by his companions.
" It made a great noise," he says, " in the country,
because I was before so remarkable for my wickedness." It exposed him, at the same time, to the
ridicule and contempt of his old associates, whose
society he now abandoned. They derided him. When

---

* " If the Lord tenders you the gift of righteousness through Jesus
Christ, do not say you cannot receive ; do not say you are not worthy of
it. The question is, are you in need of it ? Are you not guilty ? Receive
it as a grace. As it is certain nothing but grace can save the sinner, so
it is as certain there is nothing more unpleasing to the sinner than grace."
—*Trail.*

+ " The first device of Satan to keep souls in a sad doubting and ques-
tioning condition, making their life a pain to them, is causing them to be
still pouring and musing upon sin—to mind their sins more than their
Saviour. Yea, so to mind their sins as to forget and neglect their
Saviour. Their eyes are so fixed upon their disease that they cannot see
the remedy though it be near ; and they so muse upon their debts that
they have neither mind nor heart to think upon their surety."- *Brooks.*

they met, the invariable salutation was, " behold the whig!" Others of the soberer class, but who knew quite as little of the hidden life, advised him to cease reading religious books, or he would lose his reason. Some believed he was really mad. " By these things," says Buchanan, " I saw that the enmity between the seed of the woman and the seed of the serpent is very great, when even the show of religion"—such was his modest estimate of himself—" is persecuted with slanders and reproaches." These. trials were greatly aggravated by sore mental temptations, one of which continued for a period of eighteen months—temptations to blasphemy—and that recurred at a certain time each day. These Satanic assaults renewed his despondency, and caused deep prostration of spirit. Prayer was his resource—ejaculatory prayer in the fields, and long and earnest wrestlings in the closet. After protracted and ardent contendings at a throne of grace, he says, " I thought the Lord brought me near the mercy seat. My mouth was filled with arguments, and my bands falling off, I was wholly melted to tears. I thought this scripture came with overcoming sweetness and power to my soul, " shall I bring to the birth, and shall I not cause to bring forth." " Along with this word, there came a great calm to my soul. Before this, I was like the troubled sea ; but now I found great serenity of mind. I came away from the place more happy than if made emperor of all the world. I resolved I should live in the faith of that promise, " that God never brought to the birth that he did not cause to bring forth." But if these blasphemous suggestions are just " the fiery

darts of the wicked "—his artful device to drive an
awakened soul from God back to a condition of gloomy
despair; does he not as certainly seek to effect the
same thing when he assails the weak and anxious
one with powerful solicitations to self-righteousness ? We have a natural proneness to this. We
have a constitutional tendency to legality—to put our
own in place of the finished work of the Lord Jesus.
But, at the same time, there is little doubt, that in
many minds this tendency is greatly intensified by
Satanic influences. He knows our natural and constitutional proneness, and diligently and artfully works
upon it—specially when the awakened one has but faint
glimmerings of the "new way." Accordingly, we find
that in consequence of Buchanan's imperfect views of
the way of salvation by grace, he was no sooner
delivered from the fore-mentioned temptation than he
was assailed by powerful solicitations to self-righteousness. For example, we find at this period such
entries as the following.

"I thought it presumption to believe for the pardon of sin, till I should find a certain measure of
humiliation and sanctification of nature.

"I endeavoured to believe, but I could not; being
convinced it was not my duty to believe till I should
be better qualified."*

----

* "Satan would keep souls from believing, by persuading them, that
they are not qualified and sufficiently fitted for Christ, and that they have
not seen themselves absolutely lost, not so much burdened with sin as
they should."—*Powell.*
"The Spirit's work is necessary, sovereign, and effectual. But must we
feel or be conscious of the Spirit before we are warranted to believe the
Gospel ? If so, it would utterly overturn the freeness of the grace of
God; and the work of the Spirit would be so explained as to stand in
opposition to the work of Christ. In my view, there is scarcely a clearer

While longing for pardon and peace, he does not perceive that the very first step towards realising these, is to come to Jesus—to come to Him at once—to come to Him just as he was, with all his guilt and all his unworthiness—the only qualifications an unsaved sinner can have—and that as such, the blessed Redeemer is willing to receive him. He was, however, permitted to struggle on in this state of mind, until, by experience, he was taught the hopelessness of realizing in himself, and of himself, what he calls " being better qualified to come to Christ." Accordingly, under date, February 1742, we have the following entry :—

" Despairing to make myself more fit for Christ, I endeavoured to roll my soul upon Him as a poor, miserable, blind, naked sinner, without any qualification in myself to make me desirable in His sight. In this I found the outgoings of my soul towards Him. I saw Him to be in every way suitable for a lost and undone sinner. I found also some love kindled in my heart. Yet, while I had some peace in my mind, which I never had before, I still hankered after qualifications to be first wrought in me, before I could take comfort from the Saviour." So strongly does the spirit of self-righteousness cling to Him. Nothing but the grace of God can subdue it. In this condition,

proof of the necessity of the Spirit's work, to show us the true grace of God, than this continual propensity in us, to pervert it, or mistake it, and to aim at placing even the consciousness of the Spirit's work between a free Christ and our souls."—*Brief Thoughts on the Gospel.*

" As to your complaints, I humbly presume to be somewhat peremptory in saying that the sick should go to the Physician—the blind to Him that opens the blind eyes, and the dead to Him who is the resurrection and the life. Further, I must be bold to say that they who feel no sense of anything have a right to go to him to give them sense."—*Dr Love.*

oscillating between self and Jesus, he disclosed his case to a Christian woman, in whose piety and intelligence he had confidence. Of this interview he gives the following record :—

"She desired me to apply to the free and absolute promises of the new covenant.

"I said that I could not do it, as I had no qualifications to render me worthy.

"She replied that God never looked for any worthiness in the creature—that it was only for Christ's sake that we were accepted, not for our own ; and that the offer of grace was altogether free, and upon the lowest possible terms—' without money and without price.' (Rev. xxii. 17).

"I said there was a willingness and thirsting required in that invitation, which I could not find in myself; and therefore how could I come ?

"She said that even willingness was not in us by nature—for we are altogether unwilling to come to Christ—and therefore the promises of the new covenant are absolute. They don't in the least depend upon the creature's doing. 'Thy people shall be made willing in a day of thy power.' She further observed, in reference to the conditional promises, that Christ had fulfilled all these for us ; and that believers were now under a better covenant than Adam was.*

---

* "For a day or two of this week my mind was a good deal impressed, in consequence of a small tract which Mr Gentle gave me, called "Brief Thoughts on the Gospel." It met one hindrance to the reception of the gospel, which I entertained. I said, "I feel I cannot believe, it seems an impossibility. How then can I receive the offer of the gospel which I acknowledge to be perfectly free?" The author insists that the mind is here taken up with examining its own feelings, not in looking to the object, namely, Christ ; and that this is virtually denying the freeness of the gospel, as it makes our consciousness of possessing faith the condition

She also explained to him the nature of justification by faith, and directed him to the confession of faith, and shorter catechism—' in which she said he would get sound knowledge.' "

He was greatly cheered by this conversation. He found his heart, as he expresses it, going out after Christ in all his offices. " I thought also that I loved this way of salvation. I found mourning for sin which I had not before, and my love to God's people was greatly increased." " But I had still a secret hankering after the law, and wished for a righteousness of my own." He was now in his twenty-sixth year, and compares himself to the man who had his eyes half-opened, and saw men as trees walking.

July 1742.—On the second Sabbath of this month the sacrament was dispensed at Muthil. Thither he went to dedicate himself to the Lord at His table. The ministrations of Mr Halley were much blest to him.

From Muthil he went, soon after, to Cambuslang. A remarkable work of grace was progressing there under the ministry of Mr M'Culloch, Mr Whitefield, and others. " I was greatly comforted by hearing people narrate their religious experiences to one another. On the Sabbath there was a great multitude gathered. Such a sight I never saw. Mr

---

on which we will accept the gospel offer, instead of at once laying hold of it. I must indeed acknowledge this to be true. I have been all along looking too much into the state of my own feelings, and examining whether I had faith, and lamenting the want of it, instead of contemplating the glorious object Himself, or of endeavouring to bring my own mind to bear upon the unconditional freeness of the gospel, and its suitableness to my needs. Instead of coming to Christ by fixing my eye upon Him, that so I might be drawn to Him, I have been engaging myself in ascertaining how to come."—*M'Donald's Life.*

Whitefield lectured from Matt. xix., and there was an uncommon concern among the people." *

From Cambuslang he went to Comrie, to the sacrament. Here he heard Mr Halley of Muthil. He discoursed from Matt. v. "The Lord helped me to make application of the third and sixth verses. But not many days after, I raised all the foundations —thinking it was a delusion." About this time, he found a treatise on the doctrine of Justification by Faith, which helped him greatly. It showed the different views people had of Christ when closing with him for salvation. The author remarks, "that the first actings of faith are variously described in the Bible, such as looking unto Jesus—coming to Christ— fleeing to the city of refuge—running into His name, as into a strong tower—committing the soul into his hands—and trusting in His name,—so that the first actings of faith in the soul may vary. Some have

* Mr M'Culloch of Cambuslang was born at Whithorn, in Galloway. He was educated at the Universities of Edinburgh and Glasgow, and distinguished himself for his attainments in classics and mathematics. He was licensed to preach in the year 1722. On the 29th of April 1733 he was ordained minister of Cambuslang—about five miles from Glasgow. Though eminent for learning and piety, he was not eloquent. But he preached the truth of God faithfully, as his son says. In works of charity he was singular; in labours very abundant. On his death-bed he said, "The whole is summed up in this, 'He that believeth and is baptised shall be saved, and he that believeth not shall be damned.'" He died on the 18th December 1771, in the forty-first year of his ministry. The following inscription is on his grave-stone: "He was holy in his life, esteemed in his congregation, and honoured of God to be remarkably useful in preaching the gospel."

Mr M'Culloch says from a writing now before me, dated 27th April 1751: "I find a list of about four hundred persons who were awakened here in 1742, and who have been enabled to behave in a great measure as becometh the gospel.

"The number present at the three tents on Sabbath was so great that, as far as I can hear, none ever saw the like in Scotland since the revolution, or anywhere else on a sacramental occasion. The lowest estimate I hear of with which Mr Whitefield agrees, makes them to have been upwards of thirty thousand."

clearer views of Christ, and are enabled to believe in Him more strongly.   Others are weaker in faith.   As the manslayer, hasting for his life to one of the cities of refuge, was ordered to flee to that which was nearest to him, so it is the duty of sinners to flee immediately to Christ, and to that in Him, of which they have the clearest discernment ; and which in that respect is nearest to them.   Though the distinct actings of faith may vary, yet in the main they agree ; inasmuch as it is in the one Christ they believe for justification of life.   They all flee to the one Christ, the one refuge, and so are safe.   " This passage," he says, " was the means of showing me several mistakes into which I had fallen."

From Comrie he went to Kilsyth.   " On Monday," he says—the Monday after the communion—" I was suddenly enlarged in prayer, and my soul was drawn out after a whole Christ.   I came away rejoicing in the Lord and in His goodness."

But the clouds returned after the rain.   " I soon became vain and proud of my duties.   The Lord did not suffer my pride to swell.   He discovered to me the iniquity that was in my heart, which was the means of humbling me in the dust.   He blasted my gifts.   I could scarcely ask a blessing on common mercies.   He withdrew from me in some measure His restraining grace ; and left me to wrestle with my heart idols.   Then arose such a darkness and deadness in my spirit, that I could not think, desire, or do anything."   This, he thinks, was a chastisement for spiritual pride.

" Was greatly encouraged by reading Philip. i. 6.

Being confident of this very thing, that he who has
begun the good work in you, will perform it into the
day of Jesus Christ."

January 2nd., 1743.—A memorable day in Buchanan's life—"The Sabbath," he says, "on which
the Lord opened my eyes to see the Mediator in all
his offices, from 1 Cor. i. 30 ; but of him are ye
in Christ Jesus, who of God is made unto us wisdom,
and righteousness, and sanctification, and redemption."
He makes no mention where he was, or who preached,
or whether it was simply from reading the passage, that
he found such a clear light on the fulness and freeness
of Christ ?   He speaks of this occasion in terms that
would almost lead us to suppose he had light now for
the first time.   It is certain, however, that by means
of this passage, whether privately or in the house of
God, he had discoveries of the mediatorial glory of
Jesus, such as he had never previously realised. He had
his relapses after this—"thorns in the flesh, lest he
should be exalted above measure by the glory of the
revelation," but his self-righteous tendencies never
afterwards obtained their former ascendancy.   Speak-
ing of this triumph of grace, he says, "that Sabbath
evening after I had spent the greater part of the day
in meditating upon the fulness that is in Christ, I saw
how suitable He was for my case in every way, and, as
it were, called for my former unbelief, to see if it
could object anything against this complete Saviour,
now revealed to me in the gospel ; but at this time
unbelief durst not appear.   I have many a time called
the fore-mentioned scripture my charter for the heavenly
inheritance."

" I had my ups and downs after this, till the 6th of February 1743. Being Sabbath day I went to our church. My heart warmed with love to God ; but found that woeful enemy self increasing in my heart. This is the enemy that mingles water with my wine continually. It robbed God of the glory of his grace, and me of the comfort which I might have enjoyed." *

After he had gone to bed that evening, he took Ezek. xvi. 5, 6, as the subject of meditation. His soul was filled with seraphic joy as he surveyed the wonders of redeeming mercy. " O the love I saw in this chapter is far beyond anything that I can express ! When I saw, as it were, the compassionate Jesus passing by me, when I was wallowing in my blood, and saying unto me, live; this was indeed a time of love to me a vile worm. When He saw me bound in the pit wherein there was no water, He set me free by the blood of the everlasting covenant. O boundless love ! I only draw a vail over it, when I begin to speak on the subject. O my soul, come and be swallowed up in admiring this love; this boundless love to thee the chief of sinners ! O my soul wonder at the freeness of it—free without any merit. O my soul, was it anything he saw in thee, that made Him to love thee; and not only to love thee, but take thee to Himself in a marriage covenant ! Be astonished O ye heavens at this love ! O ye angels, behold the wonderful match ! O ye saints and redeemed of the Lord, whose near and peculiar privilege it is not only

* From 1724 till 1772 the Rev. Finlay Ferguson was minister of the parish of Balquhidder.

to view the match, but to be the bride, the Lamb's wife, O come and view the love that is between you and your husband ! 'For thy maker is thy husband, the Lord of Hosts is his name; and thy Redeemer the Holy One of Israel, the God of the whole earth shall he be called.' Isa. liv. 5. O my soul, be ashamed to meet such a husband, in the filthy rags of thy own righteousness. Accept of the robe that is offered thee in the gospel, for it is that robe, and none other, that will render thee acceptable in the sight of God." *

He was so absorbed in admiration of God's love in Jesus that sleep departed from him. Next morning he went to the fields to pray and praise. His joy " was unspeakable and full of glory ;" and ever after-wards, when recording what on these occasions he felt, he was so full of admiration of God's love that he could not write.

" *Sabbath evening, 6th February* 1743, was a night much to be remembered. I enjoyed sweet com-posure of mind till Thursday night ; when a vail was drawn over these things, to teach me that I was to live by faith and not by sense."

" *22d February* 1743.—When I was going to prayer I was in an especial manner taken with won-derful admiration at the freeness of divine grace to me, the vilest of His creatures."

" *26th March* 1743,—was set apart for fasting and

---

* "I am pained at wondering at new opened treasures in Christ. O that time would post faster, and hasten our long looked for communion with that fairest, fairest among the sons of men ! He hath lit a fire in my heart that hell cannot cast water on to quench or extinguish it."— *Samuel Rutherford.*

humiliation in private, for my unsuitable carriage since my bands were loosed; and also because I intended to go to the sacrament of the Lord's Supper at Glasgow."

This year he went to Kippen, the residence of earlier times; and where he heard the communion was to be dispensed. It was a happy season for him. He had sweet manifestations of God's love, and great delight in the preaching of the word, "by which," he says, "the secrets of his heart were made manifest." On the evening of the communion Sabbath he resorted to a glen, where, in former and less happy times, he was wont to pour out his heart to God. He perused the seventeenth chapter of the Gospel by John, and meditated on the contrast between his present and former devotions in the same place.

"Formerly, they consisted in working out a righteousness of my own; but the exercises of this day were directly contrary to them. A better righteousness than my own was revealed to me; for which I cheerfully renounced my own rags, and accepted of it as being infinitely better. My former exercises were forced. But this day I found the love of God in Christ constraining me to holy obedience; and believing in, and trusting to, the righteousness of Christ, made me work more than when I had in view to be justified by my works." He returned to Ardoch in a happy frame of mind, "rejoicing in the Lord and his goodness, which I had seen and felt. But in case I should be exalted above measure, there was a thorn in the flesh, a messenger of Satan sent to buffet me. For after I came home, I found great wandering of heart in time of duty ; and also blasphemous thoughts concerning God and the covenant of grace." On account of these things he set apart a day of fasting and humiliation ; and drew out a form of covenant in order to dedicate himself anew to God.* A month before he entered upon this transaction he fixed upon a day, and wrestled with God that " he would show him his covenant," Ps. xxv. 14. The day he fixed on was the 5th of August 1743. He began by reading Guthrie's trial of a saving interest in Christ, and what he considered the scriptural warrant for personal cove- nanting with God. He then sang the 51st Psalm, and prayed, " confessing his sins, and naming them as far as he could remember them." He then searched them out one by one, and found that though it should be said unto him, " if thou wilt enter into life keep the commandments," he could by no means do it. " I found myself guilty of breaking every one of them, either in heart or life, and with heinous aggravation, which rendered me the chief of sinners."

" Now, O Lord, I do here stand before Thee, a law- condemned, a self-condemned sinner, owning myself to have come short of every duty which is required, and guilty of every sin that is forbidden in thy holy law ; and therefore I will justify thy righteous judg- ment against me, even shouldest thou sentence me to the lowest hell, for it is my just reward."

" O Lord, thou wouldst do me no wrong, if this

* " As a fast-day is a day to lose the bands of wickedness, so it is a day for coming explicitly into the bond of the holy covenant. ' Going and weeping they shall go and seek the Lord their God, saying, Come and let us join ourselves to the Lord in a perpetual covenant that shall not be for- gotten.' " Jer. i. 4, 5.—*Rev. Thomas Boston.*

should be my everlasting habitation, among devils in the unquenchable flames. Thou art just and righteous, and thy law holy, just, and good, and in token thereof I do as in Thy presence, subscribe with heart and hand, guilty, guilty to Thy whole law.

" DUGALD BUCHANAN."

Having thus confessed his guilt before God, and having, as he says, spread the black catalogue of his sins before the Lord, declaring that he was a hopeless creature in himself, he proceeds thus :—

" Therefore upon the warrant of Thy offer, and in obedience to Thy divine command, I, a poor sinner, do take hold of that covenant—the covenant of grace —for life and salvation, believing on the name of Christ crucified the head thereof, and exhibited unto me as my great High Priest, who by the sacrifice of Himself, hath made atonement, and brought in an everlasting righteousness for poor sinners. Accordingly, I trust in Him, that He with his righteousness will be mine ; that in and through Him, God will be my God to make me happy here and through eternity.

" And now, O my God, I do here this day renew my baptismal engagements, to renounce the devil, the world, and the flesh ; and take all things about me to witness that I will, by Thy grace assisting me, break all my covenants with death and hell. I will have no other lords but Thee.

" I renounce all my sins ; and particularly my beloved idol.

" I renounce all subjection to Satan's government.

" I renounce all dependence on this present world ; for all my treasure is in Thee, Oh ! blessed Jesus.

C

"O, my God, I do by Thy grace acquiesce in that covenant, as all my salvation and all my desire.

"And seeing thou art a consuming fire to all who meet Thee 'out of Christ, I do therefore make choice of God in Christ as my God and portion for time and for eternity.

"Yet not I but Thou hast chosen me; and it is by virtue of Thy choosing me that I have chosen Thee.

"Oh! my covenanted God in Christ, this day I give my hearty approbation to this glorious method of salvation by Jesus Christ. I do here accept of the laws and terms of the covenant, particularly that which excludes boasting for ever, and suffers no flesh to glory in Thy presence.

"O God, the Holy Ghost, I accept of Thee as my sanctifier, guide, and comforter.

"O Lord, I appeal to Thee, who art my witness, that this is the consent of my soul; and in confirmamation of this my assent and consent to all the terms of the covenant; I do subscribe it with my hand, heart, and soul, and that God is true in the record he hath given of Christ. I set to my seal there is life in Him, and no where else.

"DUGALD BUCHANAN.

"At the Cave of this Rock,
    "August 6, 1743."

"Before I left this place, my closed lips were opened; and my mouth filled with the high praises of my God. My chains and fetters fell off; and I was set at liberty. O that was a sweet day unto my soul, when I sat in the cave of the rock, and the Lord proclaimed His name in Christ, and made all his goodness to pass before me."—Ex. xxxiv. 6.

Buchanan was at this period in the twenty-seventh year of his age, and living at Ardoch, but how employed we have no means of ascertaining. He found time, however, to make occasional excursions to neighbouring parishes, where the Sacrament of the Supper was being celebrated. These were times of refreshing to him, as the following entries show :—

"I went next Sabbath to the Port of Monteith to receive the seal of the covenant. So I received the seal of the everlasting covenant ; and before I arose from the table, with what grief, joy, and wonder did I behold my dear Redeemer bruised under the Father's wrath, which justly belonged to me.

"After that I went to Kilsyth. On Sabbath morning I heard Mr Robe preach the action sermon from Rev. i. 17, 18.* I never felt more of the power of God than I did on that occasion. Afterwards I reviewed my whole exercises from the day in which I was first awakened, to that moment ; and saw that the foundation of my peace was built upon the rock of ages ; and then with the foolish virgins fell asleep for some time, until the Lord sent a messenger of Satan to buffet me."

"His iniquities prevailed against him." He thought all his former experiences a delusion. He was ashamed, and afraid even to pray. He said to

---

* The Rev. James Robe was son of the Rev. Michael Robe, of Cumbernauld. He was settled at Kilsyth in 1713, and died in 1755. He was a learned, holy, and conscientious servant of Christ, and the Lord owned his ministry in a remarkable manner. His narrative of the revival which took place there, shows much of his character and labours.

himself, can such a power of sin be in any person who
is converted ?   He was, he says, in greater trouble of
mind now, than at his first awakening.   He wrote a
friend, to whom he unfolded his case.   From the
reply he received he saw his error, and that his temptation was sent because of the following reasons :—
Restraining prayer before God—to reprove his sloth and
security, and to teach him the danger of unwatchful-
ness.   "I saw that Satan allures me to the ways of
sin and folly, and then turns accuser.   The only way
to overcome temptation is to resist the very beginnings
of sin in the heart.   'Resist the devil and he will
flee from you.'"

From Nov. 1743 till March 1744, these troubles
remained.   But about the beginning of March 1744,
the Lord began to restore his peace as a river.   "But
I see," he says, "that no sooner one trouble goes, than
another comes in its room, and a greater."

August 1745.   "The Sacrament of the Lord's
Supper being about to be dispensed in a neighbouring
congregation, I went there, and got a soul-refreshing
view of Christ at his own table, both in a way of correction and comfort,—these Scriptures being presented
to my view.   Ezek. vi. 9 ; Amos ii. 13.   At evening I went to secret prayer ; and if ever I was sincere
in anything, it was in dedicating myself to the service
of God.   Yea, I was made to believe that he accepted
me in the beloved ; therefore, I concluded that my
mountain stood strong, and that I should never be
moved.   But little did I think, what storm was
coming, and what a journey I had to go before I was
to get another meal—no less than two whole years."

The storm referred to here was occasioned as follows :—
Buchanan's native district of Balquhidder was notori-
ously favourable to the Stuart dynasty. In the rebellion of 1745, they rose in a body, and joined the
standard of Prince Charles Edward. Dugald Buchanan's friends and relations were of the number,
and it so happened that most of them were left in
garrison at Carlisle, which was captured by Charles on
his well known expedition to England, after the victory of Prestonpans. Carlisle was subsequently taken
by the Royal forces ; and the Highlanders made pri-
soners of war. They were tried, and condemned to
death as rebels. " Though the cause was bad, says
Buchanan, yet I was heartily grieved, and could not
forgive those who, by their power and false witnesses,
were instrumental in their death ; and, by degrees,
I began to entertain resentment against them. The
devil seeing me harbour revenge, added fuel to the
flame, by representing the pleasures of being revenged
on such persons. Though they were entirely beyond
my reach, yet the thought thereof was very pleasant
to me. Sometimes, conscience would fly in my face
with this or the like Scripture, " dearly beloved, avenge
not yourselves, but rather give place unto wrath, for it
is written, vengeance is mine." But I would not
hearken to Scripture or reason. Nothing would satisfy
me but blood. Therefore I spoke favourably of that
sin, though contrary both to my reason and judgment.
I acknowledge to my own shame and to the glory of
God's patience, that He bore long with me before He
let loose Satan, and my own heart upon me." This
distress he ascribes to his having harboured those

sentiments of revenge.   He was deserted of God—
bereaved of the comforts and joys of his salvation.   He
was tempted to the foulest sins—sins which he hated
with his whole heart.   " O, the hell that I carried in
my bosom ; what Christian can hear of my dismal case,
and not tremble.   Yet this was my situation from
August 1748 till July 1750.   It was, and ever will be,
a wonder to me, in what way my soul was held in life
during these two last years ; or how any spark of
grace was left without being drowned by the enemy
coming in like a flood upon my soul.   Yet I found
my soul every now and then groaning for deliverance,
saying, " O Lord, I am oppressed, undertake for me."

June 1750.   I began to search the Scriptures more
carefully to see if there was any of the saints ever in
the like condition ; which might be a ground of hope
to my soul.   There I found it written, "I will not
execute the fierceness of mine anger, I will not return
to destroy Ephraim.   Is Ephraim my dear son—is he
a pleasant child, for since I spoke against him, I do
earnestly remember him still ; therefore, my bowels
are troubled for him."   But although I endeavoured
to make a close application of this to my own case,
yet my soul refused to be comforted.   God's time to
comfort had not yet come.   "Who is he that saith
and it cometh to pass, when God commandeth it not."

July 22d, 1750.   I got intimation that the Sacrament was to be dispensed at Muthil.   That was the
place in which my soul was first made to lay hold on
Jesus Christ ; and where I was often instructed and
comforted by the ministry of the word.*   Mr Gillespie

* After the revolution, the Presbytery of Auchterarder was enjoined to

of Carnock preached from 2 Cor. iv. 8, "We are troubled on every side, yet not distressed." The reading of the text was a sermon to me. He showed what distresses and perplexities arise from remaining corruption; and the subtlety of Satan, and why they are not in despair by all the devil, the flesh, and the world can do. I was melted down under the sermon, and thought all my bands were loosening, and the clouds dispelling. But immediately Satan raised an objection, that such a person as the minister described could not be a child of God. One other link added to Satan's chain, and he would have devoured me. But God who is all eye to see, as well as all ear to hear, and who knows my frame, remembered that I was dust. On my way home I sat down to rest, and in a minute's time, all my doubts were dispersed. The gates of brass, and iron bars of unbelief were broken in a thousand pieces, and my captive soul set at liberty.

15th December 1750.—There has not been a day since the 26th July, in which I have not experienced something of God's love and power. When I got time to reflect upon what God had done for my soul, the first thing I sought to know and examine was, that which I apprehended to be the grand cause of all those miseries which came upon me these two years past. I concluded it was harbouring revengeful thoughts against those who had injured me. At the

---

look out for a minister for the parish of Muthil. Their choice fell upon Mr Halley. He was ordained in 1704. His ministry extended over a period of nearly fifty years. There were many revivals under his Ministry, and many souls gathered to the fold of the beloved Redeemer. The writer of the New Statistical Account of Muthil says, that in 1837, the name of Mr Halley was still embalmed in the traditional recollections of the people, which shows what a deep mark his ministry left upon the public mind.

same time I found the following marks of being a be-
liever :—

First, I was convinced of the universal depravity of
my nature.

Second, I found that I had received Christ in all
his offices.

Third, I found that I had a high esteem and regard
for the holy law of God.

Fourth, I found that my obedience flowed from a
principle of love to God.

Fifth, I was reconciled to all mankind, without a
grudge. These are some of the evidences I had of
the grace of God being in me.

His diary closes in the year 1750, not long before
he began his work at Rannoch, the most eventful
period of his life in the Master's service. He con-
cludes with the following reflections and petitions, so
expressive of his humility and entire resignation to
the divine will :—

" It is not for me to know the reasons thou hast
reserved in thine own hand ; therefore send snow in
summer, or rain in harvest ; give bread of adversity,
or water of affliction ; take away one of my comforts
to-day, and others to-morrow ; do thy whole pleasure
with me and mine, and by thy grace I will say, 'Good
is the will of the Lord.'

" Cross my will, turn my wisdom into foolishness ;
my strength to weakness, when I lean on them and
not on thee ; and let all thy counsel stand fast, and
let mine fall.

" O Lord, punish me not by giving me my own
will. Hear my heart, my soul, and my faith, but O !

reject my other passions, though they cry mightily unto thee.   I do this day enter a protest in the hand of my Advocate in heaven, at God's right hand, that they be not heard ; and I promise, in the sight of God and the holy angels, and take my conscience and all about me to witness, that I shall observe thy will, that I shall not fight, nor pray against it, but submit. Save me from myself, for I am my greatest enemy.

" Now, Lord, let the dedication of myself to thee, and my accepting of thee as my God in Christ, and my being the subject of thy spiritual work, be like the day that is past, and cannot be recalled again.   Let it be ratified in heaven, and I will sign it on earth.

" DUGALD BUCHANAN."

CHAPTER IV.

" They that be wise, shall shine as the brightness of the firmament ; and they that turn many to righteousness, as the stars for
ever and ever."—DAN. xii. 3.

BUCHANAN'S diary, minute in recording the conflicts
and triumphs of his soul, contains little personal incident.　He appears to have lost sight of the one in
the all absorbing interest of the other. , Even his
marriage is but incidentally alluded to ; and in consequence of a sore illness, and the thought of leaving a
loving wife and a pleasant child, which, he says, " was
very hard upon me.　But I got over this difficulty,
being enabled to act faith upon the following scripture, ' leave thy fatherless children and I will preserve
them alive, and let thy widows trust in me.' "　This
was in 1750.　It was therefore sometime in the previous year that he must have taken this step in his
domestic history.　This is corroborated by the follow-

ing entry in the baptismal records of the parish of Balquidder :—

"8th March 1750, John, son of Dugald Buchanan
and Margaret Brisbane, in Ardoch."

Mrs Buchanan was a daughter of Mr Alexander
Brisbane, land steward to the Earl of Loudon at
Lawers,● near Crieff.   She was a worthy helpmate,
endowed with superior social and domestic qualities,
as well as sincere personal religion.   The entry also
shows that at the period of the birth of their son,
Buchanan was still resident at the paternal farm of
Ardoch.   Probably his father was by this time gone
the way of all the earth ; and tradition says that
Dugald succeeded him in the farm and mill.   From
what cause we know not ; but not long after the birth
of his eldest child he ceased his connection with the
mill and farm of Ardoch.   Indirect allusions in his
diary would lead.us to suppose that he met with disappointments and reverses in his circumstances which
obliged him to do so, and betake himself for a liveli-
hood to the work of teaching the youth of his native
district. ᛫ This is probable, for he must have had
some previous experience in this work, to recommend
him to the Barons of Exchequer for the district of
Rannoch.   His poetic gift, as we see from allusions in
his diary, showed itself at an early period ; but it was
after he began teaching that he composed and recited
certain sacred songs which attracted attention, as compositions of more than ordinary merit.   Whether
these earlier productions included any of those now in
print, we have not been able to ascertain.   But their
excellency and his eminent piety attracted the

attention of Christian people, and in their estimation
marked him for a larger sphere of usefuluess; and
sometime previous to 1753—the exact date we have
not ascertained—he was appointed schoolmaster at
Drumcastle in the district of Rannoch.

According to an ancient custom or law which it is
difficult now to explain, we find portions of our Scotch
parishes situated in the very centre of other parishes.
Thus, Drumcastle, though territorially within the
bounds of the parish of Fortingal, belongs ecclesiasti-
cally to the parish of Logierait,—from the church of
which it is over thirty miles distant, and about twenty
miles from the parish church of Fortingal, of which
parish most of Rannoch forms a part. The extreme length of the parish of Fortingal from east to
west, is about forty miles, and the extreme breadth is
from thirty to thirty-five miles. Rannoch runs
parallel with Glenlyon, and extends from the northern
base of Sith-Chaillin on the east, in a westerly
direction, upwards of thirty miles. The breadth from
north to south in several places is nearly twenty miles.
The lairds of Rannoch were then enthusiastic sup-
porters of the Stuart dynasty, and in 1745 they,
together with their men, joined the standard of Prince
Charles Edward. On the suppression of the rebellion
they had to suffer the consequences. Robertson, of
Struan, " The Bard," as he was called—conspicuous
for his zeal on behalf of the fallen Prince, was one of
the first on whom the arm of the law fell heavily.
His extensive estates were confiscated to the Crown,
and Mr William Ramsay was appointed by the Barons
of Exchequer to bring the revenues into the public

treasury. Who Mr Ramsay was, beyond the incidental notice of him in the following extract, we know not. But it is to his credit that he had the discernment to see the worth, and secure the services of such a man as Dugald Buchanan. Rannoch needed him. A wild, lawless spirit was abroad, little restrained, far less subdued, by living Christianity; and Dugald Buchanan — eloquent in address, evangelical in doctrine, full of zeal for the salvation of souls—was the very man to do the work to which Mr Ramsay and a higher than he had called him. Right nobly, by the blessing of God, was the work done.

The following extract is from the records of the Presbytery of Dunkeld, and is the earliest notice of his appointment, which we have been able to trace :—
"Dunkeld, May 1, 1753.—Mr Dugald Buchanan, who is employed by Wm. Ramsay, factor, appointed by the Barons of Exchequer upon the estate of Struan, as schoolmaster at Drumcastle, parish of Logierait being present, attending the Presbytery, produced his testimonials, with which the Presbytery were well satisfied; and he declared himself willing to submit to the directions of the Presbytery, according to the Word of God, the Confession of Faith, and the rules of this church."

"*Eodem die.* The committee appointed to examine Mr Dugald Buchanan reported that they had obeyed that appointment, and were satisfied with his knowledge and sufficiency for his office, which the Presbytery considering, they recommend it to him to be as diligent and useful in his station as possible."

Buchanan is said to have been one of the teachers

of the Society for Promoting Christian Knowledge.
But as far as appears from this extract, he seems at
the outset to have been simply a teacher of youth, invested with no functions beyond the duties of schoolmaster. At this period, therefore, his evangelistic
labours among the people were unofficial, and unre-
warded, save in the pleasure he felt in winning souls;
and a very abundant field for such work there was in
the sphere which in the providence of God was
assigned to him. Previous to the period of his settlement there, Rannoch was in an uncivilized and
barbarous condition, under little restraint of law.
For example, one of the principal proprietors never
could be compelled to pay his debts. Two messengers
were sent from Perth to give him a charge of horning.
He ordered a dozen of his retainers to bind them
across two hand-barrows, and carry them to the Bridge
of Kynachan, a distance of nine miles! His estate
abounded with thieves and cattle-lifters, who laid the
whole country from Stirling to Coupar-Angus under
contribution; obliging the people to pay them black-
mail, as it was called, to save themselves from being
plundered. Rannoch was the centre of this kind of
traffic. In the months of September and October,
they gathered sometimes to the number of 300, built
temporary huts, drank whiskey all the time, settled
accounts for stolen cattle, and received balances.
Every man bore arms. It would have taken a
regiment to bring a thief to task. Even as late as
Buchanan's settlement there, the country was im-
passable for want of bridges. The condition of the
population was miserable. Their houses were mere

huts, that went by the name of "stake and rise."
One could hardly enter on all fours, and after entering
it was difficult to stand upright. The common people
had no such thing as beds in the modern sense. They
lay on the ground with heather or ferns underneath.
A single blanket was all their bedclothes, with their
garments rolled under their heads for a pillow. Such
is the account the late Mr M'Ara of Fortingal, gives
of his parishioners about the middle of last century,
then applicable, as we suppose, to not a few out-
lying Highland districts. Mr M'Ara says that
such was the scarcity of food, that the people
bled their cattle several times a year—boiled the blood
mixed with meal, and eat it as a substitute for bread.
He knew of a poor man who supported a large family
for a whole year with a boll of meal for each of them,
prepared in this way. May we not ascribe much of the
sheep stealing and cattle lifting of past times in the
Highlands, to this condition of semi-starvation? Such,
then, was the field assigned to Dugald Buchanan, "to
make the wilderness and the solitary place glad, and
the desert to rejoice." When God has a special work
to do, he raises up men qualified for it; and the first
pioneers of evangelical truth in the Highlands were
men peculiarly fitted and gifted for their labours,
which often required real heroism to face and carry to
a successful issue. The General Assembly of the
Church of Scotland demanded from Mackintosh of
Mackintosh a bond of security for the personal safety
of Mr James Leslie, the first Presbyterian minister
settled in the parish of Moy. Mr Leslie was an able
and zealous man. The first Sabbath after ordination

to his new charge, he found his parishioners amusing themselves near the church "putting the heavy stone." On proposing that they should go to the house of God, one of them, franker than the others, said, "if the minister would try his hand at their work, then they might be disposed to listen to him." Leslie was a powerful man. He knew that he did not risk much in measuring strength with any of them who challenged him. So he took the stone, and at the first throw outdistanced all his rivals. For a little while this trial of strength was continued—as Mr Leslie wished to let them do their best. When it was again his turn he took the stone, and putting forth his whole might he threw it far beyond the foremost of them, into a deep pool in a stream hard by. There was an end to the strife. The minister had no equal, and in obedience to his wishes they all went into the church. From that day the cause of presbyterianism and evangelism was on the ascendant in the parish of Moy.

It appears that, from a very early period, both in England and Scotland, the practice of turning the day of rest into a day of profane amusement was a common one. The Book of Sports, issued by King James in 1618, and re-issued by his son Charles in 1633, though it did not originate these Sabbath pastimes, sanctioned them ; and at the same time prohibited the authorities from interfering with them. The intense religious fervour of the second Reformation banished such practices from many districts, but in remote parts of the country they continued to maintain themselves, or were revived after being suspended. Accordingly we find that, at Anwoth, when Samuel Rutherford was settled there, this habit of profaning the Sabbath was rife, as it was at Rannoch when Buchanan began work there, and at Moy at the time of the settlement of Mr James Leslie.

Rutherford was settled at Anwoth in 1627. There is still a piece of ground shown on the farm of Mossrobin, in that parish, where the people assembled on Sabbath to play football. He repaired to the spot—warned them of their sin—called the inanimate objects around them to witness against them, should they slight the warning, especially two large stones hard by, which have ever since born the name of " Rutherford's witnesses." The following lines, from the pen of Mrs A. Stuart Menteith, express beautifully the burning words which this holy man addressed on this occasion to his careless parishioners :—

" But if that thing ye bear within,
For which a God came down to die,
That washed in blood, or foul in sin,
Must share His own eternity !
If shrinks in every guilty breast,
Even as I speak, that conscious guest.
Upon your souls the charge I lay,
Ye spurn not at the Sabbath day.

" My Master's grace this day hath given,
That even the dead His voice may hear,
And now as sinners unforgiven,
I summon you to turn and fear !
And these grey stones on either hand,
God's witnesses between us stand,
If this my warning be withstood,
That I am pure from your soul's blood.

" The wood receives him from their sight,
His thrilling tones are heard no more,
Words are but words ! the day is bright,
On with the pastime as before !

D

But these grey watchers standing by,
Assume their witness silently,
And a strange awe, the boldest own,
Rebuked in presence of a stone !

" O ! conscience is a wondrous thing,
When God awakes it in its might.
The undying worm, whose full grown sting,
Through lost eternity shall smite.
A bulrush in the Spirit's hand,
Becomes a sceptre of command ;
As sands, outstretched by God's decree,
Bind the illimitable sea."

The condition of the people of Rannoch at the time
of Buchanan's settlement among them was very much
the same as that of the people of Anwoth ; and anec-
dotes of a similar kind are told of them.   Resident as
many of them were, twenty or thirty miles from the
parish church ; and with only occasional religious services, once a month, or once in three months, as the case
might be, there is little wonder if they lapsed into a state
of semi-heathenism. We may therefore believe the traditional story, that the day of rest was made a day of
amusement ; and that, on the first Sabbath after his
appointment as teacher, Buchanan found the people
playing foot-ball instead of going to the house of God.
Similar things are being done in other lands not very
distant, at the moment we pen these lines. We remember, when on our way to church in Paris, on a
Sabbath morning, the painful impression made upon
us by seeing tradesmen busily plying their work in
building and beautifying the streets of the city. Notwithstanding the imperfections of dear old Scotland,
we thanked God at the remembrance of the Sabbath
rest, that then pervaded the plains and valleys of our

native land.   Buchanan remonstrated with the people, and sought to persuade them to join him in the worship of God as more becoming the day of rest, than their sinful amusements.   He prevailed upon a few to join him that very day.   In the course of a year, these Sabbath pastimes were entirely discontinued, and such an interest awakened in divine things, that the schoolhouse of Drumcastle could not contain all who came to hear the word of God.   In good weather they met on the banks of the Tummel ; and there is a mound still there, on which Buchanan is said to have stood, while addressing the crowds that came to hear him. His services at this time were accompanied with remarkable power.   There was a deep and wide-spread revival among the people—probably the reason why the Dunkeld Presbytery invested him with the functions of catechist and evangelist, as we find from the following entry :—

" Dunkeld, May 7th, 1755."—Two years subsequent to his first appointment,—" some members of presbytery proposed that Dugald Buchanan, schoolmaster at Drumcastle, should be examined , in order to his being recommended to the Committee to be appointed by the ensuing General Assembly for managing the Royal Bounty, to be employed by them as catechist at his present station.   The Presbytery examined him, and did judge him fit to be so employed, and agreed to recommend him accordingly."

Buchanan was now invested with the responsibilities of an office, the duties of which he had previously discharged, though not officially recognized.   This recognition of him by the Presbytery gave a new impulse to his zeal. It also added somewhat to his slender pecuniary resources.* In Dr Hyndman's report of the state of religion in the Highlands, given in 1766, we find Mr Alexander Irvine, schoolmaster at Lawers, had a grant of only twenty shillings sterling a-year, with fifty or sixty scholars to teach. As catechist and evangelist, Buchanan prosecuted his work among the people with even more than his former zeal; and, in the following year, we have the Presbytery's attestation and approval again affixed to his work as evangelist.

"Dunkeld, December 7th, 1756.—Dugald Buchanan, schoolmaster and catechist at Drumcastle, was attested as to his diligence and attendance on said offices, and certificates thereof were appointed to be given him." He left no record of this period of his life. How much he could have told us, that would have been interesting had he continued his diary! In the absence of any written record by himself, the general voice of tradition, as well as the testimony of individuals who died within the memory of persons still living, go to show that his labours were remarkably owned in the conversion of souls, as well as the edification of the people of God. The following anecdote shows what power accompanied his preach-

* During a protracted winter storm, Buchanan was warned by his wife that their store of fuel was fast disappearing. His answer was, "the Lord will provide," and in dependence on Him who supplies all our need, and, not taking much thought about fuel, he prosecuted his evangelistic labours. Time passed; the severe weather continued, the peats were disappearing fast, and by and by there remained but a few days' supply. At the end of these days, his wife came to him saying, she had no fuel to prepare their next meal. His reply was, "the Lord will provide." At the very time he and his excellent wife were thus conversing about it, three young men presented themselves, who informed Dugald, that there was a raft of wood for fuel for him at the foot of the lake, which they would have floated down sooner but for the storm. Dugald said to his wife, "did I not tell you the Lord would provide!"

ing. He occasionally had meetings at the head of
Loch-Rannoch, where there was then a large population. Those were the days of feuds and petty ani-
mosities between tribe and tribe. From what cause
we know not, but there was such a bitter feud between
the people of two contiguous districts in this part of
Buchanan's district, that they could not trust themselves in close proximity, even to hear the word of
God. And yet, singularly enough, both parties were
willing to hear the evangelist. Buchanan took his
stand on a large stone in the channel of the stream
that divided the contending parties; and, from this
position addressed his audience. The address of that
day was so powerful, so owned of the Lord, that the
people were quite melted down. They confessed their
faults mutually, and that very day parted as friends.
This is an example of Buchanan's power of touching
an audience; and, in this instance, an audience little
prepared by previous training to receive impression.
By a series of such triumphs, this man of God gradually wrought quite a revolution in his field of labour.
" Instead of the thorn came up the fir tree, and instead
of the briar, came up the myrtle tree." Nor did he
confine his labours to his own district. The writer
remembers an aged relative, now gone from earth, who
used to speak with great fervour of a missionary tour
made by Buchanan in company with a man of the name
of M'Alpine, to the Bracs of Glenmoriston—the memory
of which was fragrant while that generation lasted.
The summer season, when the people were gone with
their cattle to their sheilings among the hills, was
usually his time for making these welcome excursions

to remote and dark localities, visits that were as cold water to many a weary thirsty traveller Zionward.

This rising tide of popular favour was the occasion of jealousy on the part of certain members of Presbytery—particularly as the people of Rannoch made a proposal that he should be ordained as missionary among them, and invested with ministerial functions. Buchanan himself had no hand in this movement.   It was the spontaneous outburst of popular appreciation of a man of piety and gifts, whose labours were blessed to them, and who was doing more of the work of a pastor there, than the clergyman to whom the district territorially belonged.   Those whose interest it was to resist such a proposal, sent reports to the Convener of the Royal Bounty Committee, not at all favourable to the evangelist.   He was represented as stepping beyond his sphere, and as assuming ministerial authority.   Moreover, it was hinted that his public teachings were of a wild inflammatory character, fitted to fanaticise rather than to edify.   So easy is it for jealousy and envy to invent injurious and unfounded charges against the very best of men.

About this time, associated with the Rev. James Stewart of Killin—father of Dr Stewart of Luss, Buchanan was employed in publishing an edition of the New Testament in Scotch Gaelic.   Previous to the year 1767, the Irish translation of Bishop Bedell and O'Donell was the one in use in the Highlands.   In 1754, Mr R. Kirke published an edition of O'Donell's Irish New Testament in Roman letter, more intelligible to the Gaelic-speaking people, than the Irish character. But the Irish idiom and spelling were retained.   To put the Highlanders, therefore, on a level with their Irish brethren, a new translation into Gaelic was imperatively demanded. Mr Stewart performed his work in an able and scholarly manner—showing thorough acquaintance with the idiom and vernacular of the Gaelic language. Dugald Buchanan was quite abreast of the Gaelic scholars of his time ; and he superintended the work while passing through the press. This made it necessary for him to discontinue for a time his work at Rannoch, and to reside in Edinburgh. We have not been able to discover who at this time was Convener of the Royal Bounty Committee ; but, hearing that Buchanan was in the metropolis, he determined, from personal intercourse, to ascertain the grounds of the fore-mentioned charges. He accordingly invited Buchanan to his house. These interviews resulted entirely in his favour ; and the Convener wrote the complainants, that he thought highly of Buchanan's talents, piety, and religious sentiments, and that he would willingly sit at his feet to learn Christ. During his stay in Edinburgh, he frequently addressed the Highlanders there in their native tongue, and it is said with results similar to those of his Rannoch ministrations. There was at that time no Gaelic church in Edinburgh, and so highly did the Highlanders appreciate Buchanan's gifts, that they proposed to have him settled there as minister of a Gaelic congregation. With this view, he attended classes at the University while superintending the work of the printers as mentioned above. The Church declined, however, to dispense with the usual curriculum, and the proposal was not carried out.

It, is, however, an interesting fact, that the first nucleus
of a Gaelic charge in the Metropolis was formed by
Buchanan—a charge over which so many able and
excellent ministers have since presided. ｜Whilst in
Edinburgh, Buchanan was introduced to many of the
celebrities of the city—among others, to David Hume
the historian.   It is said Hume enjoyed the freshness
and originality of Buchanan's conversation, and conde-
scended to have a chat with the Rannoch schoolmaster
concerning the beauties of authorship.   Hume observed, it was impossible to pen lines more impressive
or sublime than the following by the great dramatic
poet, Shakespeare :—

> " The cloud-capt towers,
> The gorgeous palaces,
> The solemn temples,
> The great globe itself,
> Yea, all which it inherits shall dissolve,
> And like the baseless fabric of a vision,
> Leave not a wreck behind."

Buchanan admitted the beauty of the passage, but
added that he could quote a passage from another
author, which even the philosopher himself would
admit to be superior to that of Shakespeare.   Hume
smiled incredulously.   He probably thought he knew
pretty well all that could be said on the subject,
but requested that the passage should be repeated.
Buchanan recited with solemn emphasis the words
of Revelations xx. 11-13.

> " I saw a great white throne,
> And Him who sat on it,
> From whose face the earth and heaven fled away,
> And there was found no place for them.
> And I saw the dead small and great

Stand before God.
And the books were opened.
And another book was opened,
Which is the book of life.
And the dead were judged out of those things
Which were written in the books,
According to their works.
And the sea gave up the dead which were in it.
And death and hell gave up the dead which were in them.
And they were judged each man
According to their works."

It is said that Hume acquiesced in Buchanan's estimate of this passage of Divine writ, and that he asked
who the author was ; quite probable, as the philosopher, conversant as he was with general literature,
was perhaps not very familiar with the sacred writ-
ings.

While engaged in printing the Gaelic New Testament, Buchanan made arrangements to publish the
first edition of his Sacred Songs.   Much interest has
been shown, and research made, as to when these
poems were composed.   This we have no means of
knowing.   Some of them are supposed to have been
composed before he went to Rannoch.   The late Rev. Mr
M'Donald of Fortingall, in his Statistical Account, says,
Buchanan was the author of several poems besides his
printed ones ; and that the latter were but specimens
of a larger collection, which he intended to publish
had his life been spared.   It is likely, therefore, that
they were composed at different periods and in different places.   Some of them were the productions of an
earlier period, but two of them at least—" The Day
of Judgment" and "The Skull"—were composed
after he went to Rannoch.   The following anecdote
favours this opinion.   A friend of the name of

Kennedy, a teacher in the upland part of the district, was a frequent guest at Buchanan's humble but hospitable dwelling. They usually slept in the same apartment. On one of these occasions, and in the dead of night, the stranger was aroused by the inquiry, " Are you asleep, Kennedy ? " " Why do you ask ? " was the reply. Buchanan, who was at the time composing " The Skull," and thinking it over, even " in the night watches," answered, " Shall I say *Duragan dónn* or *Duragan cróm ?* " brown worms or crooked worms. Kennedy, not thinking this a sufficient reason for disturbing his repose, replied hastily, " Either, as you please ;" but, on second thoughts, added " *duragan cróm.*" Buchanan rose, lighted a candle, wrote for a little while, then returned to rest. Kennedy frequently told this anecdote after his friend was gone to be with the Master, but always with self-accusation, because he had spoken so hastily on a subject that so deeply occupied the thoughts of the beloved and admired author. The incident also shows, that while genius produces its rare fruits, it is also a laborious and painstaking faculty ; and that, as a rule, excellency in any pursuit is not attained without diligence and close application. We remember seeing a manuscript of the celebrated poet—Alexander Pope—in the British Museum. It was the MS. of one of his most admired productions, the stanzas of which flow as easily and mellifluously in print, as if they had cost no effort to the author. But the interlined, corrected, and re-corrected manuscript told its own tale. In fact, it is difficult to say which are the original lines, so multifarious are the changes and corrections

in course of careful and fastidious preparation for the
public eye. It appears from the above incident, that
Buchanan bestowed extraordinary pains in order to
perfect in expression, as well as thought, these admirable productions of his. The first edition was published
in 1766. He did not live to see a second. He died
two years after of an epidemic fever that was pre-
valent in the country. The fever was a lingering one;
and he was frequently delirious. While his mind
wandered, he often repeated with great fervour
favourite passages of Scripture—especially that which
describes the Lord Jesus as " the Lamb in the midst
of the throne." In lucid intervals, he expressed his
full, firm hope of salvation through the redeeming
blood of Jesus, and his desire to " depart and be with
Christ." He had had dangerous illnesses before this,
and as he had survived them, hopes were entertained
that he would outlive this malady. But this was not
the Lord's will. The summer was hot, the fever was
virulent, and he sank under it some day in June
1768, at the comparatively early age of fifty-two
years. His death made a deep impression, and
caused profound sorrow. Every family in the district
mourned as if one of their own number were taken
away. Fourteen years of Dugald Buchanan as schoolmaster and evangelist, had wrought a change among
the people of Rannoch ; and not a few of them
realized how sore a loss they had sustained by his
removal. Venerating him, therefore, as they did, it
was natural they should wish to have his remains
interred among them ; but his friends at Balquhidder were desirous that he should be buried there.

The Highlands were then but emerging from barbarism, and the contention on this point was such that there was danger of violence.   But the grief at Rannoch was so great, and the people so subdued by a sense of their loss, that they laid aside their opposition.   The Balquhidder men were permitted quietly to bear away the remains and bury them in the burying-ground of Little Leny.

The following is from the Rev. Mr Findlater of Lochearnhead, the respected Free Church pastor of Buchanan's native parish, and who knows the localities he describes intimately.

"FREE CHURCH MANSE, LOCHEARNHEAD,
"18th December 1874.

"My dear Mr Sinclair,—In answer to your letter, I am sorry that I cannot give you even 'scraps' in regard to Dugald Buchanan, as the people here do not seem to me to have the same love of traditionary lore as our friends of the north Highlands have. But I will answer two of the queries you put, to the best of my ability.

"The river Balvaig flows from Loch Voil into Loch Lubnaig; and is about four miles in length. By the way, the Gaelic name Balvaig is very characteristic of Highland nomenclature—it being a word-picture of that dumb and sluggish stream.

"The churchyard of Little Leny is on the bank of the Teith. It is a square built place of interment —I should say not above twenty feet square. It is only persons of the name of Buchanan who are buried there. I was once inside of it ; and saw the grave of

Dugald Buchanan. The building may be seen from the window of the railway carriage, on the left hand just after crossing the bridge going north. It is one of the many clan cemeteries so common in Perthshire. As they could not agree on earth, they were resolved to offer no temptation when under it !

" The mill is still a working mill at Ardoch; but it is likely it has been rebuilt since Buchanan's time. I believe what now is the schoolhouse was the place of Dugald's birth. It is opposite the Railway Station at Strathyre, and very near the spot where it was proposed last year to erect a monument to his memory.

" I wish you every success in editing Dugald Buchanan's works. He was a true poet, and a Christian of a type of which we have too few now-a-days. —I am, yours faithfully, ERIC J. FINDLATER.

Buchanan left a widow, two sons and two daughters to mourn his loss. His widow survived till 1824, and one of his daughters was alive as lately as 1854.

The following letter from Mr Ferguson of Raploch, one of the surviving relatives of Buchanan, will be read with interest :—

RAPLOCH, STIRLING, 24th Nov. 1873.

DEAR SIR,—As the latest discovery I have made in reference to Buchanan is freshest in mind, I will begin with it. I recollect when you were here, we both had the impression that his mother was a Ferguson. I think I have made out conclusively the names in full of his father and mother. Let me tell how, and leave you to judge for yourself. I got a friend to search the parochial registers of Balquhidder, in the Register Office, Edinburgh, and he found that in 1716, there were three of the name of Buchanan at Ardoch—namely, Patrick, John, and Robert, and their wives. On getting this information, I called for Buchanan's great grandchildren in Callander, and asked if they knew the name of Buchanan's father. They answered, they thought it was John. I asked if it could be Patrick or Robert, and they said no. I then got my friend in Edinburgh to search for the registration of Dugald Buchanan's own family; and he found two entries—

" ' 1750, March 8th.—Dugald Buchanan and Margaret Brisbane, in Ardoch, had a child baptized and called John.'

" Here is additional evidence of his father's name; for it is highly probable, that he called his first-born after him.

" The name of the wife of the elder John Buchanan, was Janet Ferguson—of the same family of Fergusons to which I myself belong. There are still in Balquhidder a family of the name of Ferguson, connections of the poet's mother, who have a bed and press once belonging to Buchanan. The press is said to have been made by his own hands.

" Another item of interest found in the parochial registers is as follows :—' 1757, May 10th.—Dugald Buchanan and Margaret Brisbane, his wife, had a son baptized and called Alexander.' Comparing dates, it would appear from this entry, that Mrs Buchanan did not accompany her husband at the date of his removal to Rannoch. Probably domestic arrangements did not permit of it for some time.

" I think I mentioned to you when here, that I lately learned from a very old friend in Balquhidder, that Buchanan was a teacher in his native parish—that he itinerated at one time in Strathyre, then in the Braes of Balquhidder, and at another time in Lochearnhead.

" Regarding his family, after his death, I learned the following from his descendants at Callander.   The eldest daughter was brought up in Leny house near Callander, and was married out of that house to a Mr Lawson, some of whose descendants are still living. He was ten years of age at the time of Buchanan's death ; and he often told his grandchildren still living the spot where his father-in-law was buried.

" The youngest daughter, born after her father's death, was married to a gamekeeper in the service of the Duke of Montrose.   She was a Mrs Kirke, and died in 1854, at the age of eighty-five years.   Another daughter lived in a gentleman's family near Dumfries, and was married to a Major Campbell.   His only surviving son is said to have learned his father's trade, that of a house carpenter.   He was long in delicate health, and an Edinburgh gentleman of the name of Reid, is said to have shown him much kindness on account of his father.

" I think I told you the Lawson family in Callander have the press in which Buchanan kept all his papers. It is in as good a state of preservation as ever.

" The cave, or rather the rock which he mentions in his diary, is a conspicuous object from the village of Strathyre.   The glen to which he was in the habit of resorting for praise, prayer and reading of the Scriptures on Sabbath evenings, could be no other than

Glenbuckie. There is a footpath from beside the spot
where he was born, to Glenbuckie—a path which I
myself have often trod in days gone by, inasmuch
as I was brought up in Glenbuckie—and the nearest
path to Callander and Stirling. Buchanan was a
grand traveller. The distance between Kippen and
Strathyre was nothing to him. When resident at
Kippen, at his trade, he was frequently at Strathyre
on the Sabbath, having tripped along by hill and dale
on Saturday evening. Meantime I do not recollect
anything further that you are not aware of. Kindest
regards.—Yours very respectfully,

                              ROBERT FERGUSON."

The following testimony to Buchanan's merit, is
from the pen of the late Rev. Robert Macdonald of
Fortingal :—" Dugald Buchanan was another eminent
character connected with this district—a valuable man
in his day, and highly useful in enlightening the
people in the knowledge of the truths of the gospel.
In his manners among his intimate acquaintances, he
was affable, free, and jocular. He was consequently
much esteemed, both by gentlemen, and by the common people of the district—who, when they had not
an opportunity of hearing sermon from the parish
minister, flocked to him on Sabbaths, when he read
and expounded the Scriptures to them. He was a
severe disciplinarian, feared, but at the same time beloved, insomuch that the people offered to raise a fund
to send him to college, and become their pastor in the
district, on the Royal Bounty. But from some cause
or other, the plan was not followed out. Dugald

Buchanan was the author of a small but valuable collection of sacred poems, in the Gaelic language, which displays poetical talent of no ordinary kind. They are to this day admired and read with benefit, by every Christian who understands the language. He composed several songs on various subjects, that were never published."

Sometime subsequent to the rebellion of 1746, the Sutherlandshire militia were stationed at Dunkeld. A detachment, consisting of twelve men, was sent to Rannoch to see to the loyalty of the people, whose Jacobite proclivities were more than suspected. The Sabbath after their arrival, they inquired where they could hear the word of God preached or read. They were told that Mr Dugald Buchanan, schoolmaster, was in the habit of addressing all who chose to hear him. · They went to Dugald's meeting-house. These men knew the gospel, as they were accustomed to hear it preached in their native country ; and some of them were sincere believers in the Lord Jesus. They saw at once that Buchanan was an excellent godly man— having clear comprehensive views of divine truth. A close intimacy sprung up between them. Two of them, Andrew and Alexander Ross, had a great attachment to Dugald Buchanan ; and they had frequent meetings for Christian fellowship. At these interviews, the Rosses used to recite spiritual songs composed by John Mackay, a Sutherlandshire bard. Buchanan, whose memory was as remarkable as his other gifts, soon picked them up, and sang them with great spirit. Andrew Ross used to say of Dugald Buchanan, " that he was as tender, as kind, as warmhearted a man,

E

in addressing sinners from the word of God, as he ever saw or heard."*

In personal appearance Dugald Buchanan was above the average height, of dark complexion, dark hair, and large expressive eyes. In his later years he wore knee-breeches, a blue greatcoat, and a broad blue bonnet. In earlier years he wore the kilt—the common dress of the country. In this dress he frequently attended the communion at Glenlyon. Even ministers in those days officiated in the Highland costume. The writer's father remembered the late Rev. John M'Donell of Forres, preaching to the people of his native glen—Glenmoriston—in a kilt surmounted by a black coat ! The late Rev. Malcolm Nicolson of Kiltarlity usually wore the kilt, and officiated in this dress. Times and manners have changed since those days.†

Buchanan's Spiritual Songs are full of good poetry. The celebrated Dr Samuel Johnson is said to have made the observation, that it was hazardous for a poet to attempt Bible themes, lest his strain should fall

---

.·* Rose's "Introduction to Mackay's Sacred Songs."

† Mr M'Donell in his statistical account of Forres, in 1796, writes as follows. The extract shews, how greatly within a comparatively short period, our social habits have changed, and material wealth increased :— "About fifty years ago there were only three tea-kettles in Forres; at present there are not less than 300. The blue bonnets of Forres were then famous for good credit, and at that period there were only six people with hats in the town ; now about 400. About 30 years ago 30s. would have purchased a complete holiday suit of clothes for a labouring servant. About the year 1750 a servant engaged for harvest had 4d. a day with his victuals, now 10d. with two meals. A woman servant then had 8s. 4d. and some 10s. half-yearly, now from 18s. to 21s. Beef and mutton sold in the markets at a penny per lb. and fish at a penny per dozen." The progress our country has made since then—seventy-nine years ago, is equally great. Let us not forget how much of this we owe to the blessed gospel ; which in every way, "is the power of God unto salvation."

beneath his subject.   There is little doubt that, in
many instances, the observation is quite applicable.
But it is not the case with Dugald Buchanan.   We
rise from the perusal of his poems with our thoughts
of divine things elevated more than ever.   For
example, what a vivid idea he gives of the vastness of
divinity, when he tells us that in their efforts to comprehend it, men and angels are as one who tries—

> " To contain the ocean in a mussel shell."

Or again—" Though the sun, and the system which
revolves round him, were extinguished, they would no
more be missed from the works of God than a drop of
water from the great ocean."—"Sileadh meòir."   The
late Dr Chalmers has a similar idea in his celebrated
sermon on astronomy, where he says, that the extinc-
tion of a globe causes no more sensation among the
innumerable worlds that people infinite space, than
the fall in a forest of a decayed autumnal leaf.   How
beautiful and true the following—

> " The smallest letter of the name of God—
> 'Tis a heavier load than human reason can sustain."

Who has not felt the indescribable oppressiveness
that weighs upon us when attempting to grasp the
infinite !

Take again, the description of the resurrection in the
" Day of Judgment," the gathering of the scattered
remains of the untold myriads entombed in the crust
of our earth, and the tumult caused by the rapid re-
union—" bone coming to its bone "—

> " Bithidh farum mòr am measg nan cnàmh
> Gach aon diubh dol do àite féin."

Or the colloquy between the spirits of the lost and
their risen bodies is very powerful—quite in the style
of Danté, and little if at all inferior to that great
master of the terrible, in the strains of the poetic
muse.   Equally vivid is his picture of the surprise of
Pilate, as he beholds the great Judge of the universe
seated upon his throne of majesty, and identifies him
with the very Jesus whom he condemned at his
tribunal—

> " 'Us thusa Philat tog do shuil,
> 'Us faic a nis am mugha mòr,
> An creid thu gu'r E sud au Tì,
> A rinn thu dhìteadh aìr do mhòd."

How terrible the power of the Judge to take vengeance
on his enemies, and crush them-—

> " He holds a thousand thunders in his hand, —
> His foes in wrath to crush,---
> That long to be let loose,
> As hunter's hounds to be let loose upon their prey."

"The Dream," is replete with striking passages.   It
is hardly possible to select.   How true the allusion to
the unsatisfactoriness of life's pleasures—"the rose
which we no sooner pluck, than both its hue and
odour disappear."   Or when he reminds the ambitious,
"that the sighs of a monarch are as many as those of
the lowliest subject."   Or when he compares men's
attempts to escape life's ills, to the efforts of one to
straighten a crooked staff — "No sooner do you
straighten the one end, than the bend is transferred
to the other."

The hero is not the conqueror of men or kingdoms,
but he in whom grace reigns, and by grace conquers.
Alexander and Cæsar were not heroes ; for while they

subdued others, they remained the slaves of their own
lusts. There are many beautiful passages in this
poem. For example, how small and insignificant, in
the light of eternity, are the unceasing labours and
struggles of restless worldlings who, " like ants on an
anthill, trample on each other, and quarrel fiercely
about a little fibre of broken wood—"

" A null sa nall gun fhois gun tàmh,
A tional as gach àit do'n cist.
Gu lionmhor marcachd thar a chéil,
Sa trod gu géur mu bhioran brist."

"The Skull" is by many reckoned to be Buchanan's
best poem. He passes in review the beautiful maid
—the judge—the physician—the general—the epicu-
rean—the landlord—and the minister of the gospel.
The skull may have been that of any of them. This
idea he works up, in language the most powerful and
graphic—describing their character as fancy depicts
it, and as illustrative both of their former condition
and deeds, as well as of their future destiny, as the
case may be. The conception of this poem is quite
original, and shows, in no ordinary degree, the power
of creative genius. This poem alone would have made
Buchanan famous among Highland bards.

The last of Buchanan's poems is " The Prayer "—
full of the richest devotional feeling and evangelical
sentiment. What can be more beautifully expressive
of the sufficiency of atoning blood to shield us from
wrath, than the following—

" Gidheadh am fíod au lasair féin,
A sgoilteas as a cheile 'n tuil,
Drùghadh orm fo ùmblachd Chriosd,
'S mi gabhail dion a steach fo fhuil."

The idea is in Ex. xii. 3. Again, how beautifully his own interest in this atoning blood, is expressed according to the words of Rom. iii. 25, in the following stanza. It contains whole volumes of theology—

> " An fhuil a dhiol do cheartas teann,
> 'Sa dhortadh air a chrann gu lar,
> 'S ann aisd' tha m' earbsa O mo Righ,
> Nach dìt thu m' anam air a sgàth."

Numerous conversions have resulted from reading these poems and hearing them recited. It was formerly the custom, in many a Highland hamlet, to gather round the domestic hearth in winter, or on the village green on Sabbath evenings in summer, to hear a village patriarch read or sing one or other of these poems. We have it on good authority, that not a few have been thus gathered to the fold. "Singing the gospel" is not a new thing. The Ephesians "spoke to themselves in psalms, and hymns, and spiritual songs." The following letter, from our esteemed friend Dr Maclauchlan, shews with what good results this was done. by singing the Spiritual Songs of Dugald Buchanan :—

                              "EDINBURGH, 14th Dec. 1874.

" My dear Mr Sinclair,—I am sorry that I can add little to what is generally known of Dugald Buchanan. It is now so long since his death, that all which was carried down by tradition has been gradually lost ; and little remains but what was written. His own autobiography is the best memorial of him which we possess ; and, I need hardly add, how creditable it is both to his religious character and his literary power. I may add my item to the testimony universally borne by Gaelic scholars to his poetical merit. There is not in any language truer poetry than that to be found in the sacred songs of Buchanan. They are throughout, the offspring of sanctified genius, and commend themselves to the admirers of such, wherever the Gaelic language is spoken. I have heard from a reliable source, that in the early part of this century, Buchanan's hymns were in the habit of being sung at prayer meetings in some of the straths of the "*Monadh Liath*," south of Inverness; and I have heard it further stated, that there were several eminent Christians in that part of the country, who could trace their earliest impressions of divine truth to this practice. It is undoubted, that they have been largely blessed to the spiritual edification of the Church of God. I wish you much success with your proposed re-issue of these admirable poems; and I earnestly pray that they may be a comfort and a blessing to many of our countrymen both here and abroad.—Yours very truly,

"THOS. M'LAUCHLAN."

It is not easy to decide to which of these poems we should give pre-eminence. They are all admirable, each in its own way, abounding in originality and felicity of expression seldom equalled, and never surpassed by any of our Gaelic poets. There is scarcely a verse of these sacred songs, but has obtained among our Highland fellow-countrymen, the currency of aphorisms; while the beauty of the versification, and the freshness and originality of illustration are such as cannot be forgotten by any one who has perused them in the original. Necessarily, on account of the subjects of them, they abound largely in Bible thought. But even when Buchanan borrows, there is a charm about his manner of utilising his materials, of which it is sufficient to say, that he does no discredit to the sacred originals.   He is equally happy when he borrows from the scenes of nature, or draws his illustrations from the facts and occurrences of every-day life.   In his use of them, he shows admirable skill.   They sparkle through his verse like gems—unperceived, and unappreciated by others, but which he, with rare powers of observation, and tact, seizes upon, separates from their baser surroundings, causes to reflect light, to inform the mind, and to pin to the memory of the reader, the great truths of salvation and immortality.

We will not attempt a critical analysis of his performances.   Our Gaelic readers do not require it at our hands.   The English reader we leave to judge for himself from the translations we have given.   At the same time, we must premise that no translation can do full justice to poetry, especially high-class poetry. Its power and pathos depend so much on idiom, as well as on the language in which the original is composed, that in course of translation, much must necessarily be lost.   At the same time, we are not without hope, that even with these disadvantages—specially true of a translation from Gaelic to English,—so much of the original will remain, as that Dugald Buchanan's sacred songs will not be unacceptable or unprofitable even in a foreign dress.

Drumcastle, where he began work, is about a mile to the east of the village of Kinloch-Rannoch on the north bank of the Tummel.   Subsequently, he removed to that village, where he resided till his death.   His cottage, a drawing of which accompanies this volume, is still standing and inhabited. The schoolhouse adjoined the cottage, with a private entrance to it through the gable, since closed up, but the outline of which is still visible. The cottage is a thatched dwelling, with a " but " and " ben," and a small closet between. The " ben " was his spare room. There he slept. The bed still remains. It has been carefully preserved by tenant after tenant as a relic of him who once owned it ; and whose memory is so dear to the people. It is a " box-bed," closed on all sides by fir boards, and having folding doors in front. In the day time, these doors were closed, and the apartment could be used as a parlour or bedroom, as occasion might require. We are not a worshipper of relics, but we confess to a feeling of deep veneration, the first time we looked on this plain, antiquated piece of furniture, in company with our dear friend, the late Rev. Mr M'Innes of Tummelbridge. This, we thought to ourselves, is the very bed in which Dugald Buchanan slept, in which he " meditated in watches of the night," in which he composed portions of his " Day of Judgment," in which he died, and from which his ransomed soul was borne away by angels, to join " the spirits of the just 'made' perfect," to be for ever and ever with his Lord and Master, whom he served so faithfully, and loved so well.

Dana. –

LAOIDHEAN SPIORADAIL,

DUGHALL BUCHANNAN.

MORACHD DHE.

O ciod* e Dia, no ciod e ainm,
Cha tuig na h-aingle 's àird' an glòir!
E'n solus dealrach folaicht' uath',
Far nach ruig sùil no smuain 'na chòir.

Uaith' féin a ta a bhith a' sruth';
Neo-chruthaichte ta uile bhuaidh';
Neo-chriochanach 'na nàdur féin;
'S féin-dhiongmhaltas ga 'n cumail suas.

Cha robh ᴇ òg 'us sean cha bhì;
O shior gu sior gun cháochladh staid;
Cha tomhais grian no gealach aois;
Oir 's nithe cáochlach iad air fad.

---

* In the original edition it is " cread," the Irish form of the word.

'Nuair thaisbeanas E 'ghlòir no ghràs.
Bidh là neo-bhàsmhor teachd o shùil;
'S grad chuiridh sluagh nan nèamhan àrd
Le 'n sgiathaibh sgàile air an gnùis.

'S ma' thaisbeanas E'ghnùis an gruaim,
Grad sgaoilidh uamhunn feadh nan spéur;
Roimh' achmhasan-sa teichidh 'n cuan,
'S le geillt-chrith gluaisidh 'n cruinne-cé.

Ta oibre nàduir searg' 'sa fàs,
O chaochladh tàid gu caochladh ruith:
Ach uile thionnsgain-s' 'tàid 'nan áon,
Gun tráogh' no lionadh air a bhith.

'Ta aingle 's dáoin' do neo-ni dlù;
A' bhrù o'n d'thainig sinn gu léir,
Ach iomlanachd-s' o shiorr'achd tà,
Neo-chrìochanach 'na nàdur féin.

'Nuair chuala neo-ni guth a bhéil,
Ghrad léum na bith a' chruitheachd mhòr,
An cruinne so le uile làn,
'S na nèamhan àrd le'n uile shlòigh.

'N sin dhearc' air oibribh féin gu léir,
'S gach créutair bheannaich E 'nan staid,
'S chad d' fhéum ath-leasachadh air nì,
A measg a ghnìomharra air fad.

Air clàr a dhearn' tha dol mu'n cuairt,
Gach réul a ghluaiseas anns an spéur;
'N cruthach' gu léir tha 'stigh 'na ghlaic,
'S a' deanamh' thaic d'a ghàirdean tréun.

Co chuartaicheas do bhith a Dhé!
An dóimhne' shluig gach réusan suas;
'Nan oidheirpean tha aingle 's dáoin'
Mar shligean maoraich' glacadh 'chuain.

O bhith-bhuantachd tha thus' a'd' Rìgh,
'S ni bheil san t-saoghal-s' ach nì o'n dé;
O 's beag an eachdraidh chualas dìot,
'S cha mhòr de d' ghnìomh ata fo'n ghréin.

Ge d' thionndaidh 'ghrian gu neo-ni'rìs,
'S gach ni fa chuairt a soluis mhòir;
'S co beag bhiodh d' oibre 'g ionndrain uath',
'S' bhiodh' cuan ag ionndrain sileadh 'mhcòir.

An cruthach' cha dean le uile ghlòir,
Làn fhoillseachadh air Dia nam feart,
Cha 'n 'eil 's na h-oibre ud gu léir,
Ach taisbean earlais air a neart.

Le'r tuigse thana 's diomhain duinn
Bhi sgrùdadh 'chuain ata gun chrioch;
An litir 's lugha dh' ainm ar Dé,
Is tuille 's luchd d' ar reusan ì.

Oir ni bheil dadum cosmhuil riut
Am measg na chruthaich thu gu léir,
'S a' measg nan dáoine ni bheil cainnt
A labhras d' ainm ach d' fhocal féin.

FULANGAS CHRIOSD.

'S e fulangas mo Shlànuighear
    A bhios mo dhàn a' luaidh,
Mòr irioslachd an àrd-Rìgh sin
    Na bhreith 's na bhàs ro chruaidh,
'S e 'n t-iongantas bu mhìorbhuilich
    Chaidh innse riamh do shluagh ;
An Dia' bha ann o shìorruidheachd,
    Bhi fàs 'na chìochran truagh.

'Nuair ghabht' am broinn na h-òighe E ;
    Le còmhnadh Spioraid Dé,
Chum an Nàdur Daonna sin,
    A dheanamh aon ris féin ;
Ghabh e sgàil mu Dhiadhaidheachd ;
    S de'n BHRIATHAR *rinneadh** feòil,
'Us dh' fhoillsicheadh 'n run diomhair sin,
    Am pearsa Chriosd le glòir.

---

* In the original " *dhearnadh*," the Irish word for the one
above substituted.   See the Irish and Scotch translations of
the Scriptures.   John chap. i. ver. 14.

Rugadh 'an stàbull dìblidh ᴇ,
  Mar dhìlleachdan gun treòir;
Gun neach a dheanadh càirdeas ris,
  No bheireadh fàrdoch dhò,   *dhà*
Gun mhuinntir bhi 'ga fhrithealadh,
  Na uidheam mar bu chòir:
Ach eich 'us daimh ga chuartachadh
  D' an dual gach uile ghlòir.

Mu'n gann bha fios gu'n d'thainig ᴇ
  Do dhùisg' dha nàimhde mòr:
'Us b' fhéudar teich*do'n Eiphid leis, *teicheadh*
  Roimh Herod bh'air a thòir,
Is ò cho nàimhdeil dioghaltach
  Chum Iosa chur gu bàs;
'S gu'n mharbhadh leis gach clocharan   *d'*
  'Na rìoghachd bha, gun dail.

Bha broclach aig na sionnachaibh   *Matt 8. 20.*
  Ga'm falachadh o théinn   *and*
Bha nid aig eunlaidh 'n adhair fòs   *Luke 9. 58.*
  An géugaibh àrd nan crànn;
Ach Esan a rinn uile iad,
  'S gach ni sa' chruinne-ché,   *Suggests the verse*
Bha ᴇ féin 'na fhògarach,   *in 'twas me for*
  Gun chòmhnuidh aig fo'n ghréin. *Prince Charlie':—*

                             "On hills that are
Am feadh 'sa ghabh an Slànuighear *by right his own,*
  Mar ionad tàmh an saogh'l.   *He roams a lonely*
                             Stranger" etc.

* *This cutting off the suffix is common in Perthshire.*

Mar léigh ro iochdmhor fàbharach
    Bha 'leigheas chlann nan dáoin' ;
'N aon éucail riamh bu ghàbhuidh bh' ann,
    'S gach galar cràiteach géur,
Do* thionndaidh E chum slànachaidh
    'Nuair làbhradh E o bhéul.

Thug teanga do na balbhanaibh,
    'S do'n bhacach mhall a lùgh,
Do 'n bhodhar thug E chlàistinneachd,
    'S do dhaoine dall an iùl,
Na lobhair bhréun do ghlanadh leis,
    Cur fallaineachd 'nam feòil :
Gach éucail anama leighis E,
    'S na mairbh do thug E beò.

Shearmonaicheadh an soisgeul leis,
    Do dhaoine bochda, truagh ;
'Us gheall E saorsa shìorruidh dhoibh
    Bha 'n glais fo' chìs ro chruaidh :

---

* "*Do*" is generally expressed before the verb in old Gaelic poetry, in the Past tense of the Indicative, and sometimes for no reason whatever but to add a syllable to the measure. The Editors of various editions of this work have deleted this word, and substituted words of their own in its place, by which the poetry in many instances has been transposed. We have preferred to retain the original reading.

Fulangas Chriosd

Na'n gabhta ris an fhìrinn leo,
　Le creideamh fiorghlan beò,
'S gu 'm biodh iad air an iompachadh
　'O ghnìomharaibh na feòl'.

Lean buidheann tur do'n fhàsach E,
　'Us dh'fhan trì làith 'na chòir,
Cùig mìle bha de dh'àireamh ann
　Bh'air fàilneachadh chion lòin;
'N ro bheagan fhuair iad, bheannaich E
　'N dà iasg 's cùig arain eòrn',
'Us dh'ith iad gus 'na shàsaich' iad
　'Us dh'fhàg iad ni bu leòr.

Do chaisgeadh onfhadh chuaintean leis,
　'S an tonnan uaibhreach mòr,
A ghaoth ro laidir, bhuaireasach,
　Do chuartaich E 'na dhòrn:
Ach aithris air gach mìorbhuile,
　Rinn Iosa ànns an fheòil,
Cha chumadh 'n saogh'l de sgrìobhainnibh,
　Na dh'innseadh è gu leòr.

Ach 'nuair bha 'n t-àm a' dlùthach' ris
　Gu'n siùbhladh E chum glòir,
Ghairm E thuige dheisciobuill,
　'Us dheasaich E dhoibh lòn:
Chuir E sìos 'nan suidhe iad
　'S gach uidheam air a' bhòrd;

F

Aran 'us fion do riaraich' orr'
  Bha clallach' fhuil 'us fheòil.

'Us thug E sin mar òrdugh dhoibh
  Bhi 'n còmhnuidh ac gu bràth,
A dh' fhoillseachadh 'mhòr-fhulangais,
  A dh' fhuiling air an sgà :
Gu'n itheadh 'us gu'n òladh iad
  Do dh' fheartaibh mòr a 'ghràidh,
'S gu 'm bitheadh è mar chùimhneachan
  D' a mhuinntir air a bhàs.

'N uair thainig chum a ghàraidh E
  An sin bha 'chràdh ro mhòr ;
'Nuair' fhuair E 'n cupan féirge sin,
  Bha oillteil searbh r'a òl.
Air ghoil bha' chuislc chraobhach-san
  Tre chorp ro naomh 'ga fhàsg',   *fhàsgadh,*
'Na fhalas fola' braonadh 'mach
  Tre 'aodach air an làr.

'N sin thuit E air a ghlùinibh sìos
  ` A deanamh ùrnuigh ghéur ;
"O Athair chaoimh ma's comas e
  An deoch so cuir uam féin ;
Ach so a' chrìoch mu'n d'thainig mi,
  Gu'n sàbhalainn mo thréud,
Mar sin ni iarram fàbhar, ach
  Do thoil gu bràth bhi déant'."

Be sud an cupan uamhunnach,
  Do fhuair E 'n sin 'na làimh ;
✚ Peacadh 'n t-saoghail ga chuartachadh
  'S gach duais a bhuineadh dhà.
Na dh'fhuilgeadh'n saoghal gu sìorruidheachd
  De phiàntaibh 'us de chràdh,
Chaidh sud a leagadh còmhladh air,
  'S an deoch ud dh' òl 'nan àit.

B'e 'n diabh'l a shealbhaich Iùdas sin,
  Le chridhe dùbailt' fiar ;
An cealgair sanntach, lùbach ud,
  A chuir du-chùl ri Dia :
An troiteir reic a Shlànuighear,   *traoiteir*
  'S a mhaighstir gràdhach féin,
'Us bhrath d'a nàimhde bàsmhor E
  Fo chàirdeas pòg a bhéil.

An sin do rinn iad prìosanach
  De dh' Iosa gun chion-fàth,
'Us thug iad dh' ionnsaidh Phìlat E,
  Gu'n dìteadh è chum bàis :
'Us dhìt am breitheamh éucorach
  Le fianais bhréig' an Tì,
Bha 'choguis féin ag innseadh dha
  Bhi dì-chiontach 'us fìor.

Do cheangail agus sgiùrs' iad E.
  Le buillibh drùiteach géur,

Peacadh an t-saogh'l g'a chuartachadh

An fheòil o'n chnaimh do rùisgeadh leò
   'Na meallaibh brùit gu léir,
A chorp ro naomh' do mhilleadh leò
   'S a chreuchda sileadh sìos;
An fhuil le 'n ceannaichte 'n saoghal so
   Gun sgoinn bhi dhì no prìs.

Fòs rinneadh crùn de'n sgitheach leò, *droigheann*
   'Us dh'fhigh iad è gu teann,
Chur tuille pian 'us nàire air,
   Do spàrr iad è mu cheann;
Mu' cheann a steach do bhuaileadh leo
   Na bioraibh cruaidh ro ghéur.
'Us aghaidh ghlòrmhor dh' fholaich iad
   Le 'n smugaid' salach, bréun.

'Nuair chuir iad an crun nàrach air,
   Ro chràiteach goirt do bhì,
Do sgeadaich iad le sgàrlaid e
   Cuir colbh 'na làimh mar Rìgh
'Us labhair iad gu sgallaiseach
   A' fanoid air an Tì:—
"Fàillte' Rìgh nan Iùdhach dhut,
   Le 'n glùn g'a chromadh sìos."

Le 'm foirneart mhòr do dh' éignich e
   'Chrann-céusaidh thogail suas,
Ach ge bu chruaidh sud b' fhéudar e
   Bhi 'géilleadh dhoibh san uair:

A chuisle chaomh a' traoghadh as
    'S a neart ga fhàsgadh uaith,
A' dìreadh 'n t-slèibh ga shàrach' gus   *Sharachadh*
    An d' fhàilnich E fo 'n chuail.

Sìos air an leabaidh dhòrainnich,
    Le dheòin do luidh E fèin ;
Ruisgt' air a chrann do shìneadh E,
    'S gach alt dheth spion' o chéil' ;
A chorp ro naomha beannaichte,
    Do cheangail iad gu teann,
Le tairngibh 's òrd ga 'n sparradh sud,
    Gu daingean ris a chrann.

An crann an sin do dhìrich iad,
    'Us Iosa thog air suas,
'Us air na tàirngibh chrochadh E
    Le dochann tha do-luaidh ;
A chothrom féin a' réubadh as
    Gach créuchd na chois 's na làimh,
'Us fhuil ro phrìseil naomha-san
    Ga taomadh sìos gu làr.

Ach ge bu mhaslach cràiteach leis
    Am bàs a dheilbheadh leò ;
Aon ghearan riamh cha d'thainig uaith
    An aghaidh nàimhde mòr ;
Ach 's ann a ghabh E 'n leisgeul-san,
    Ga 'n teasairginn gu fior,

"O Athair thoir dhoibh maitheanas,
　　Taid aineolach 'nan gniomh."

Chaidh dìbh-fhearg Dhé a thaomadh air
　　Gach uile thaobh mu'n cuairt,
Bha gnùis a ghràidh air fholach air
　　'Us thionndaidh' solus uaith';
'Us dh'éigh ᴇ fo n̲o pianntan sin,　　*na*
　　"Mo Dhia! Mo Dhia na tréig!
Na ceil do ghnùis ro fhàbharach,
　　'S na fàg mi ann am' fhéum."

Na 'n rachadh an tróm-dhioghaltas
　　Do ghiùlain Ios' ann féin,
A leagadh air a chinne daoin',
　　'S na h-ainglean naomh le chéil,
Do chasgradh ann a m̲ò̲m̲a̲i̲n̲t̲ bhig,　　*moment.*
　　Na slòigh ud leis gu léir:
Am bráon bu lugh' d'a fhulangas
　　Loisgeadh e'n cruinne-cé.

'Us dh' orduich Dia nan sluagh an sin,
　　Iad theachd mu'n cuairt do'n t-sliabh.
Gach uile nàdur réusanta,
　　Do rinn ᴇ féin o chian:
'S gu 'm faicte 'ghaol d'a chréutairibh
　　'S do bhéusaibh' pheacaidh' fhuath,
Anns an fheirg a thaomaich ᴇ
　　Air Mac a gháoil san uair.

'S e so bu chainnt d'a fhulangas,
  "Nis tuigibh uile shluagh,
Nàdur sgreitidh 'pheacaidh ud,
  'S am dhòruinn faicibh 'dhuais;
'Us nàdur teann a' cheartais sin
  A ghlac mi as leth chàich;
Nach maith dhomh bónn d'am fiachan-san
  'S nach dìol mi ach le m' bhàs."

Bha 'm bàs ud mallaicht', piantachail,
  Ro ghuineach, dioghaltach, dòigh;
Ro chràiteach, nàrach, fadalach,
  'S e teachd neo-ghrad 'na chòir:
Bu ni ro oillteil uamhasach,
  Sè uair' bhi'n crochadh beò
Air fèith'a chuirp gan spionadh as,
  Co dh'fheudas inns' a leòn!

Bha brìgh a chuirp air toirmachadh
  An àmhuinn féirge Dhé:
'S a chridhe càirdeil fìrinneach
  A' leaghadh sìos mar chéir:
A theanga lean r'a ghialaibh-san,
  'Bha riamh am pàirt a shluaigh;
'Us fòirneart nan géur-phianntan sin,
  A' sniomha' anama uaith.

A fhradharc glan do dh'fhàilnich air,
  'S mar ghloine dh'fhàs a shùil;

Bha téith'a chridh' a' bristeadh aig,
　'Sa bhràghad clisgeadh dlù:
A ghnùis á b' àillidh snuadh 'us dreach,
　Air tionndadh uaine lì—
Air leam gu'm faic mi 'n fheala-ghris th'air
　'Cur a chath' shéirbh gu crìch.

Air leam gu'm faic mi chreuchdan-san,
　Mar 'réub na tàirngcan fhèoil;
An fhuil fàs dubh a' ragadh ump';
　Sìor lagach' air a threòir;　　　*Lagachadh.*
Dreach a bhàis a' tional uim';
　'S e dealachadh r'a sgiamh;
Ar leam gu'n cluinn mi 'g osnaich e;
　'S a phlòsgail bha 'na chliabh.

Fa dheireadh labhair Iosa riu,
　"Tha mi an ìotadh mhòr:"
'Ghabh domblas agus fion-géur iad ̇ˣ˙
　'S deoch shìn iad dha r'a h-òl,
'N sin thubhairt,—"Tha e crìochnaichte
　Gach nì ghabh mi 'os làimh."
'S le sgairteachd ghéur do ghlaodh e 'mach
　'Us chlaon e 'cheann gu bàs.

Be sud an glaodh bha cruadalach,
　Do chual e 'n cruinne-cé;
Gach creag air talamh sgealbadh leis,
　'S na mairbh ghrad chlisg gu léir:

Do thiondaidh' ghrian gu dorchadas,
  'Us chaochail colg gach ni,
Bha chruithcachd mar gu 'm bas'cheadh i,
  'S i tàradh chum a crìch.

Na flaitheas bha riamh sòlasach
  'S na sloigh bha subhach shuas,
San àm sin rinneadh brònach iad,
  'S an ceòl do leig iad uath ;
Ri faicinn dhoibh an Ughdair ac'
  San ùir ga leagadh sìos,
Am bàs a bhi ga cheangal-san
  'Thug anam do gach ni.

LATHA 'BHREITHEANAIS.

Am feadh 'ta chuid is mò de'n t-saogh'l
Gun ghaol do Chriosd, gu'n sgoinn d'a reachd
Gun chreideamh ac' gu'n d'thig e rìs,
Thoirt breth na fìrinn air gach neach.

An cadal peacaidh taid na'n suain
A' bruadar pailteas de gach nì :
Gun umhail ac' 'nuair thig am bàs,
Nach meal iad Fàrras o'n ard Rìgh.

Le cumhachd d'fhocail Dhé tog suas,
An sluagh' chum aithreachais na thrà,
'Us beannaich an Dàn so do gach neach,
Bheir seachad éisdeachd dha le gràdh.

Mo smuaintean talmhaidh Dhé tog suas,
'S mo theanga fuasgail ann mo bhéul;
A chum gu'n labhrainn mar bu chòir,
Mu ghlòir 's mu uamhunn latha Dhé.

Air meadhon oidhch' 'nuair bhios an saogh' l,
Air aomadh thairis ann an suain;
Grad dhùisgear suas an cinne-daoin',
Le glaodh na trompaid 's àirde fuaim,

Air neul ro àrd ni f hoillseach' féin,
Ard-aingeal tréun le trompaid mhòir;
'Us gairmidh air an t-saogh'l gu léir,
Iad a ghrad éiridh chum a' mhòid:

" O cluinnibhs uile chlann nan daoin',
Nis thainig ceann an t-saogh'l gu beachd;
Leumaibh 'n'ur beatha sibhs' ta màrbh,
Oir gu dearbh 'ta Ios' air teachd."

Us seididh e le sgal cho cruaidh,
S' gu'n cuir e sléibhte 's cuan 'nan ruith;
Clisgidh na bhios marbh 'san uaigh,
Us' na bhios beò le h-uamhunn crith'.

Latha 'Bhreith333333333mais.

Le osaig dhoinionnaich a bheil,
An saogh'l so réubaidh e gu garg,
'S mar dhùn an t-seangain dol 'na gluas'
Grad bhrùchdaidh 'n uaigh a nìos a' mairbh.

'N sin cruinnichidh gach cos 'us làmh,
Chaidh chur san àraich fad o chéil:
'S bi'dh farum mòr a' measg nan cnàmh,
Gach aon diubh dol nan àite féin.

Mosglaidh na fìreanaich an tùs,
'Us dùisgear iad gu léir o'n' suain,
An anama turlingidh o ghlòir,
Ga'n còmhlachadh aig béul na h-uaigh'.

Le aoibhneas togaidh iad an ceann,
Ta àm am fuasglaidh orra dlù;
'Us mar chraoibh-mheas fo iomlan blàth,
Tha dreach an Slànuighear 'nan gnùis.

Tha obair Spiorad Naomh nan gràs
Air glanadh 'n nàduir o 'n taobh steach:
'S mar thrusgan glan 'ta ùmhlachd Chrìosd,
Ga'n deanamh sgìamhach o'n taobh 'mach.

Dùisgear na h-aingidh suas 'nan déigh,
Mar bhéisdean gairisneach as an t-sloc;
'S o ifrinn thig an anama truagh;
'Thoirt coinneamh uamhasach da 'n corp.

'N sin labhraidh 'n t-anam brònach, truagh
R'a choluinn oillteil, uabhar, bhréun,—
"Mo chlaoidh! ciod uim' an d'éirich thu
Thoirt peanas dùbailt oirn' le chéil?

O 'n éigin dòmhsa dol a rìs,
Am prìosan neo-ghlan steach a'd' chré?
Mo thruaighe mi, gu'n d'aontaich riamh,
Le d' an-mianna brùideil féin!

O 'm faigh mi dealach' riut gu bràth!
No 'n d'thig am bàs am feasd a'd 'chòir!
'N drùigh teine air do chnamhaibh iairn!
No dìbh-fhearg Dhé an struidh i d'fheòil!

Eiridh na rìghrean 's daoine mòr,
Gun smachd gun òrdugh ann 'nan làimh;
'S cha' n aithn'ear iad a'measg an t-sluaigh,
O'n duine thruagh' a bh' ac' na thràill.

S' na daoine uaibhreach leis nach b' fhiu
Gu 'n ùmhlaicheadh iad féin do Dhia;
O faic a nis' iad air an glùn;
A' deanamh ùrnuigh ris gach sliabh:

"O chreagan tuitibh air ar ceann,
Le sgàirnich gharbh de chlaehan cruaidh,
'Us sgriosaibh sinn á tìr nam beò,
A chum 's nach faic sinn glòir an Uain!"

A mach as uamha gabhaidh 'thriall
An diabhol 's a chuid ainglean féin,
Ge 'cruaidh e 's éigin teachd a làth'r,
A' slaodadh slàbhraidh as a dhéigh.

'N sin fàsaidh rugha anns˜an spéur
Mar fhàir na maidne 'g éiridh dearg;
Ag innse gu bheil Iosa féin,
A' teachd na dhéigh le latha garbh ;

Grad fhosglaidh as a chéil' na neòil,
Mar dhorus seòmair an àrd Rìgh,
'Us foillsichear am Breitheamh mòr,
Le glòir 'us greadhnachas gun chrioch.

Tha 'm bogha-frois mu'n cuairt d'a cheann,
'S mar thuil nan gleann tha fuaim a ghuth;
'S mar dhealanach tha sealladh 'shùl
A' spùtadh as na neulaibh tiugh.

A ghrian àrd-locharan nan spéur,
Do ghlòir a phearsa géillidh grad:
An dealradh drillseach thig o ghnùis,
A solus mùchaidh e air fad.

Cuiridh i uimpe culaidh bhròin,
'S bi'dh 'ghealach mar gun dòirt' oir' fuil,
'Us crathar cumhachdan nan spéur,
A' tilgeadh nan réulta as am bun.

Bidh iad air udail anns an spéur,
Mar mheas air géig ri ànradh garbh :
'Tuiteam mar bhraoin do dh' uisge dlù,
'S an glòir mar shùilean duine marbh.

Air carabad teine suidhidh E,
'S mun cuairt da béucaidh 'n tairneanach,
A' dol le ghairm gu crìoch na'nèamh,
'S a' réub' nan nèul gu doinionnach.

O chuidhlibh 'charbaid thig amach,
Sruth mòr de theine laist' le féirg ;
'Us sgaoilidh 'n tuil' ud air gach taobh,
A' cur an t-saogh'l na lasair dhéirg.

Leaghaidh na Dùile 'nuas le teas,
Ceart mar a leaghas teine céir ;
Na cnuic 's na sléibhtean lasaidh suas,
'S bidh teas-ghoil air a' chuan gu léir.

Na beanntan iargalt' nach d'thug seach,
An stòras riamh do neach d'an deòin,
Ta iad gu fialaidh taosgadh 'mach,
An iònmhais leaght' mar amhainn mhòir.

Gach neach bha sgrìobadh cruinn an òir,
Le sannt, le dò-bheart, no le fuil ;
Lan chaisgibh 'nis bhur 'n iotadh mhòr,
Sa nasgaidh òlaibh dheth o'n tuil.

Latha 'Bhreitheanais

O sibhse rinn 'ur bun de'n t-saogh'l,
Nach d'thig sibh 's caoinibh ò gu géur,
'Nuair tha e 'gleacadh ris a bhàs,
Mar dhuine làidir dol do'n éug.

A chuisle chleachd bhi fallain, fuar,
Ri mireag uaibhreach feadh nan gleann,
Tha teas a chléibh 'ga smùidreadh suas,
Le goilibh buaireis feadh nam beann.

Nach faic sibh chrith tha air mu'n cuairt,
'S gach creag a' fuasgladh anns gach sliabh,
Nach cluinn sibh osnaich thróm a' bhàis,
'S a chridhe sgàincadh stigh 'n a chliabh.

An cùrtain gorm tha null o'n ghréin,
'S mu'n cuairt do'n chruinne-ché mar chleòc,
Crupaidh an lasair e r'a chéil,
Mar bhéilleig air na h-éibhlibh beò.

Tha 'n t-adhar ga thachd' le neula tiugh,
'S an toit 'na meallaibh dubh dol suas;
'S an teine millteach 'spùtadh 'mach,
'Na dhualaibh caisreagach mu'n cuairt.

Timchioll a' chruinne so gu léir,
Borb bheucaidh 'n tàirneanach gu bras;
'S bidh 'n lasair lomadh glòir nan spéur
Mar fhalaisg ris na sléibhtibh cas.

'S a chum an doinionn atadh suas,
O cheithir àirdibh gluaisidh 'ghaoth;
'Ga sgiùrs' le neart nan aingle tréun,
'Luathach' an léir-sgrios o gach taobh.

Tha obair nan sè là 'rinn Dia,
Le lasair dhian ga cuir 'na sgaoil;
Cia mòr do shaibhreas' Rìgh nam feart.
Nach ionndrain casgradh mhìle saogh'l!

'M feadh tha gach ni 'an glacaibh 'n éig,
'S a chruitheachd féin dol bun-osceann,
Teannaidh am Breitheamh oirnne dlù,
A chum gach cùis a chur gu ceann.

'N sin gluaisidh E o àird nan spéur,
Air cathair a Mhòrachd féin a nuas,
Le greadhnachas nach facas riamh,
'S le' Dhiadhachd sgeudaichte mu'n cuairt.

Tha mìle tàirneanach 'na làimh,
A chum a nàimhde sgrios am féirg.
'Us fónn-chrith orr' gu dhol an greim,
Mar choin air éill ri àm na séilg.

Aingle gun aireamh tha na chuirt,
Le 'n sùilean suidhicht' air an Rìgh,
Chum ruith le òrdugh-san gun dàil,
'S na h-uile àit ga'n cur an gniomh.

O Iudas thig a nis a làthair,
'S gach neach rinn bràithreas riuta 'd'ghniomh,
An dream a dh'aicheadh creideamh Chriosd,
Na reic E air son ni nach b'fhiach.

A shluagh gun chiall thug miann do'n òr,
Roimh ghlòir 'us aoibhneas flaitheas Dé,
Bhur malairt ghòrach faicibh nis,
'S an sgrios a thug sibh oirbh féin.

'S a' mhuinntir uaibhreach leis 'm bu nàr
Gu 'n cluinnte cràbhadh dha nur teach ;
Faicibh a ghlòir 's na b' ioghnadh leibh,
Ged dhruid E sibh a' rìogh'chd amach.

O Herod faic a nis an Rìgh,
D', an d'thug thu spìd 'us masladh mòr,
Ga sgeudachadh le trusgan ruadh,
Mar shuaineas sgallais air a ghlòir.

Nach faic thu Breitheamh an t-saoghail gu léir
'S mar eudach uime 'n lasair dhearg ;
A' teachd thoirt duais do dhaoine còir,
'S a sgrios luchd-dò-bheirt ann am fearg.

'Us thusa Philat tog do shùil,
'S gu'm faic thu nis' a mùthadh mòr;
An creid thu gur E sud an Tì
A rinn thu dhìteadh air do mhòd ?

An creid thu gur e sud an ceann,
Mu'n d' iath gu teann an sgitheach géur
No idir gur i sud a ghnùis,
Air 'thilg na h-Iùdhaich sileadh bréun!

'M bu leòr gu'n theich a' ghrian air cùl,
A' diultadh fianuis thoirt do'n ghniomh?
Ciod uim' nach d'fhuair a' chruitheachd bàs,
'Nuair chéusadh air a chrann a TRIATH?

Cuiridh E aingle 'mach gach taobh,
Chum ceithir ghaothaibh 'n domhain mhòir
A chuartachadh gach aon de'n t-sluagh,
A steach gu luath a dh'ionnsuidh 'mhòid.

Gach neach a dh' àitich coluinn riamh,
O'n ear 's o'n iar tha nise' teachd,
Mar sgaoth do bheachaibh tigh'n mu ghéig
An deigh dhoibh éiridh 'mach o'n sgeap.

'N sin togaidh aingeal glòrmhor suas,
Ard bhratach Chriosd da'n suaineas fuil;
A chruinneachadh na ghluais sa' chòir
'S d'a fhulangas rinn dòigh 'us bun.

D'a h-ionnsuidh cruinnichibh mo naoimh,
'Us tionailibh gach aon de'n dream,
A rinn gu dìleas 'us gu dlù,
Le creideamh 's ùmhlachd ceangal leam.

Latha Bhreitheanais.

N sin tionsgnaidh 'm Breith' air cùis an là
A chum a nàimhde chur fo bhinn,
'Us fosglaidh E na leabhr'ean suas,
Far am bheil peacadh 'n t-sluaigh air chuimhn'.

Fosglaidh E 'n cridhe mar an cèudn',
Air dòigh 's gur lèir do'n h-uile neach,
Gach uamharrachd bha gabhail tàmh,
Air feadh an àrois ud a steach.

'Nuair chi'd an sealladh so dhiù féin,
'Us dearbh gur lèir dhoibh ceartas Dhia;
'S bi'dh 'n gruaidh a leaghadh as le nàir
Nach lugha cràdh na teine dian.

Togaidh an trompaid 'rìsd a' fuaim,—
"Na labhradh 'us na gluaiseadh neach;
Air chor 's gu'n cluinn gach beag 'us mòr.
A bhreth thig air gach seòrs' a mach.

" A dhaoine sanntach' thréig a' chòir,
'S a leag bhur dòchas ann bhur toic,
A ghlais gu teann 'ur cridhe suas,
'S a dhruid 'ur cluas ri glaodh nam bochd.

" An lomnochd cha do dhion o'n fhuachd,
'S do'n ocrach thruagh cha d'thug sibh biadh,
Ged lion mi féin 'ur cisd' le lòn,
'S 'ur treuda' chuir a' mòid gach bliadhn'.

" Ni bheil sibh iomchuidh air mo rìogh'chd,
As eugmhais fìrinn, iochd, 'us gràidh :
'S o réub sibh m iomhaigh dhibh gu léir,
Agraibh sibh féin 'nar sgrios gu bràth.

"'Us sibhs' bha guidheachan gu dian,
Gu'n glacadh 'n Diabh'l bhur 'n anam féin;
S mithich 'ur n-ùrnuigh fhreagra' dhuibh,
'S na abraibh chaoidh' *Gur cruaidh a' bhinn.*

"'Us sibhs' a rinn 'ur teanga' féin,
A ghéurachadh chum uilc mar sgian,
Le tuaileas, cùl-chainnt, agus bréug,
'S le toibheum tabhairt béum do Dhia.

" A nathraiche millteach 's oillteil greann,
Cha bhinn leam ceòl 'ur srannraich àrd,
'S cha 'n éisd o'r teangaidh ghobhlaich cliù
Le drùchd a phuinsein air a bàrr.

"'Us sibhs' thug fuath do m' orduigh' naomh,
'Us leis nach b'ionmhuinn caomh mo theach,
Leis am bu bhliadhna suidhe uair,
Am àros' tabhairt cluais do m' reachd.

" Cionnas a mhealas sibh gu bràth
A'm' sheirbhis Sàbaid shiorruidh bhuan
No cionnas' bheir 'ur n-anam gràdh,
Do'n ni do'n d'thug bhur nadur fuath ?

" Luchd-mì-ruin agus farmaid mhòir
Do'n doruinn iomlan sonas chàich,
Le doilghios géur a' cnàmh bhur cré
Mu neach sam bith oirbh féin bheir bàrr.

" Cionnas a dh' fheudas sibh gu bràth
Lan shonas àiteach' ann an glòir ;
Far am faic sibh mìlte dream,
Ga'n ardach' os 'ur ceann gu mòr ?

" Am fad 's bu léir dhuibh feadh mo rìogh'chd,
Neach b' àirde inbhe na sibh féin ;
Nach fadadh mi-run 's farmad cùirt,
Tein'. ifrinn duibh am flaitheas Dé ?

" 'Us sibhs' 'an slighe na neo-ghloin ghluais,
S gu sónruicht' thruaill an leabaidh phòsd' ;
Gach neach a thug do m' naomhachd fuath,
Ga'n tabhairt suas gu toil na fòol'.

" Mar b' ionmhuinn leibh bhi losgadh 'n teas
'Ur n-uabhair, dheasaich mi dhuibh fearg,
Leabaidh theth 'san luidh sibh sìos,
Am brachaibh-lìn de lasair dhearg.

" Ged bheirinn sibh gu rìoghachd mo ghlòir,
Mar mhucan' steach gu seòmar rìgh ;
Ur nàdur neoghlan bhiodh ga chràdh,
Le'r mianna bàsachadh 'chion bìdh.

" Gach neach tha iomchuidh air mo rìogh'chd,
Teannaibh sìbhse chum mo dheis,
'Us cruinnichibh seachad chum mo chlì,
A chrìonach o na crannaibh meas."

'N sin tearbaidh e a chum gach taobh,
Na caoirich o na gobhraibh lóm;
Ceart mar ni'm buachaille an tréud,
'Nuair chuartaicheas e 'spréidh air tóm.

'N sin labhraidh e ri luchd a dheis,
" Sibhse ta deasaichte le m' ghràs,
Thigibh, sealbhaichibh an rìoghachd,
Nach faic a sonas crìoch gu bràth.

" Spealg mise 'n geat' bha oirbhse dùinnt,
Le m' ùmhlachd 's m' fhulangas ro-ghéur;
'S dh fhosgail an t-sleagh gu farsaing suas
Am leth-taobh dorus nuadh dhuibh féin.

" Chum craobh na beath' ta 'm Fàrras Dé,
Le aoibhneas teannaibh steach d'a còir
'S a fearta iongantach gu léir,
Dearbhadh 'ur n-uile chréuchd 's bhur leòn.

" An claidheamh bha ruisgte laist' ga dion.
O làimh ar sinnsir Adhamh 's Eubh,
Rinn mise truaill de m' chridhe dhà,
'S a lasair bhàth mi le m' fhuil féin.

" Fo' dosraich ùrair suidhibh sìos,
Nach searg 's nach crìon am feasd a blàth ;
'S mar smeòraichean a' measg nan géug,
Chum molaidh gléusaibh binn 'ur càil.

" Le 'maise sàsuichibh 'ur sùil,
'Us oirbh fo' sgail cha drùigh an teas.
O 'duilleach chùbhraidh òlaibh slàint ;
'Us bithibh neo-bhàsmhor le 'meas.

" Gach uile mheas tha 'm Fàrras Dé,
Ta nis gu léir neo-thoirmisgt' dhuibh :
Ithibh gun eagal o gach géig,
A nathair-nimh' cha téum a chaoidh.

" 'Us uile mhiann 'ur n-anama féin,
Lan shàsaichibh gu léir 'an Dia,
Tobar na firinn, iochd, 'us gràidh,
A mhaireas làn gu cian nan cian.

" Mòr-innleachd iongantach na slàint,
Sior rannsaichibh air àird 's air lèud,
'S feadh oibrichean mo rioghachd mhòir
'Ur n-eòlas clocrach cuiribh' mèud.

" 'Ur n-aoibhneas, mais' 'ur tuigs', 's 'ur gràdh,
Bitheadh gu siorruidh fàs ni 's mò :
'S ni 'n coinnich sibh aon ni gu bràth,
Bheir air bhur n-anam cràdh no leòn.

" Cha 'n fhaca sùil, 's cha chualadh cluas,
Na thaisg mi suas do shonas duibh,
Imichibh,'s biodh 'ur dearbhachd féin,
Sior innse' sgéul duibh air a chaoidh."

Ach ris a mhuinntir th'air a chlì,
Labhraidh e 'na dhìoghltas cruaidh,
"A chuideachd nach d' thug gràdh do Dhia,
A chum an diabhoil siùbhlaibh uam.

" 'S mo mhallachd maille ribh gu bràth,
A chum 'ur cràdh 's 'ur cur fo phian :
Gluaisibh-sa chum an teine mhòir,
Ga'r ròsdadh ann gu cian nan cian."

Mar sgàin an talamh as a' chéil,
'N uair ghabh e teaghlach Choradh steach,
Ceart làimh riu fosglaidh 'n uamha béul.
'S i miananaich air son a creich.

'Us mar a shluig 'mhuc-mhara mhòr,
Iònas an uair chaidh' thilgeadh 'mach.
Ni slugan dubh an dara bàis,
A charabad iathadh umpa steach.

San uamha taobhaidh iad r'a chéil,
A ghluais 'n am beath' gu h-éucorach :
Luchd-mhionn 'us mortaidh's fianuis-bhréig;
Luchd-misg 'us reubainn 's adhaltranais.

Mar chualag dhris an ceangal teann,
An slabhraidh tha gach dream leò féin ;
'S an comunn chleachd bhi 'n caidreamh dlù,
Mar bhioraibh rùisgte dol 'nan cré.

Mar leomhan garg fo' chuibhreach cruaidh,
Le thosgaibh réubadh suas a ghlais :
An slabhraidh cagnaidh iad gu dian,
'S gu bràth cha ghearr am fiaclan prais.

'Bidh iad gu siorruidh 'n glacaibh 'bhàis
S' an crìdh' ga fhàsgadh asd' le bròn.
Ceangailt air cuan do phronnasc laist'
'S a dheatach uaine tachd' an sròn.

Mar bhàirneach fuaighte ris an sgeir,
Tha iad air creagaibh goileach teann :
'Us dìbh-fhearg Dhé a' seideadh 'chuain,
Na thonnaibh buaircis thar an ceann.

'Nuair dhùineas cadal cruaidh an sùil,
Teas féirg' 's an-dòchas dùisgidh iad ;
A chnuimh nach bàsaich 's cibhle beò,
A cur an dòrainn shiorruidh 'meud.

Air ifrinn 'n uair a gheibh iad scalbh.
'S lan-dearbhadh co do'n loc iad cls,
Faodaidh sinn 'an gearan truagh
'Chur anns na briathraibh cruaidh so sìos.

"O staid na neo-ni 'n robh mi 'm thamh.
Ciod uime 'n d' àrdaich Dia mo cheann!
Mo mhìle mallachd aig an là
'N do ghabh mo mhàthair mi 'na broinn.

"Ciod uime 'n d'fhuair mi tuigse riamh?
No ciall' us reusan chum mo stiùir'?
Ciod uim' nach d'rinn thu cuileag dhiom,
No durrag dhìblidh anns an ùir?

"Am mair mi 'n so gu saogh'l nan saogh'l!
'N tig crìoch no caochladh orm gu bràth
Am bheil mi nis san t-siorruidheachd bhuan,
A' snàmh a chuain a ta gun tràigh!

"Ged àiream uile reulta néimh,
Gach féur 'us duilleach riamh a dh'fhàs,
Mar ris gach braon a ta sa' chuan,
'S gach gaineamh chuartaicheas an tràigh.

"Ged chuirinn mìle bliadhna seach,
As leth gach aon diu sud gu léir,
Cha d'imich seach de'n t-siorruidheachd mhòir
Ach mar gu 'n tòisicheadh i'n dé.

"Ach O 'n do theirig tròcair Dhé!
'S am pian e mi gu saogh'l nan saogh'l!
Mo shlabhraidh 'n lasaich e gu bràth!
No glas mo làmh an dean e sgaoil'!

"'M bi'm béul a dh'orduich Dia chum seinn
Air feadh gach linn, a chliù gun sgìos,
Mar bhalagan-sóididh' fadadh suas
Na lasrach uain' an ifrinn shìos!

" Ged chaidh mo thruaighe thar mo neart
Gu deimhin féin is ceart mo bhìnn;
Ach c'fhada bhios mi 'n so ga m' chràdh,
Mu'm bi do cheartas sàitheach dhiom!

"No 'm bi thu dioghailt' dhiom gu bràth
'N deach lagh an nàduir chuir air cùl?
Mo thruaighe mi! 'n e so am bàs
A bhagair thu air Adhamh 'n tùs?

" Air sgàth do dhioghaltais 'm bi thu 'sniomh
Snàthain mo bheath' gu siorruidh caol?
Nach leòr bhi mìle bliadhn' ga'm losg'
As leth gach lochd a rinn san t-saogh'l?

" Ged lean do dhioghaltas mi gu m' chùl,
Cha 'n ardaich e do chliù a Dhé,
'S cha'n fhiu do d' Mhòrachd d' fhearg a chosd,
Air comhara' cho bochd rium féin.

" O Dhia! nach sgrios thu mi gu tur?
'S le d' chumhachd cuir air 'm anam crìoch,
'S gu staid na neo-ni tilg mi uat,
Far nach 'eil fulang, smuain, no gnìomh.

" Ach O se so mo thoilt'ncas féin
'Us ni bheil eucoir buntuinn rium ;
Oir dhiùlt mi tairgsc shaor do Chriosd,
S nior ghabh mi d'a fhuil phrìscil suim.

"Mo choguis dìtidh mi gu bràth,
An fhianuis bha ga 'm chàincadh riamh ;
An-iochd no eucoir ann mo bhàs,
Cha leig i chàradh 'm feasd air Dia.

" Thilg mi aithcanta air mo chùl,
'Us ruith mi dùrachdach gu m' sgrios,
'Us 'fhianuis féin a' m' chridhe mhùch,
A' druid' mo shùilcan roimh mo leas.

" Cia meud an dioghaltas dhomh 'tha 'n dual
As leth mo pheacaidh uamharr dàn !
Am peac' thug dubhlan do dh'fhuil Chriosd,
'S a dh'fhàg gun eifeachd brìgh a bhàis.

" Gidheadh nach 'eil do Bhuaidhean féin
Neo-chrìochanach gu léir o chian?
'S an toir mo chiont air iochd, 's air gràdh
Gu'm fàs iad crìochnaicht' ann an Dia?

" An comas dut mo thilgeadh uat
Far nach cluinn do chluas mo sgrcad ?
'M 'bheil dorchadas an ifrinn féin
Far nach léir do Dhia mo staid ?

" A' d' aoibhneas iomlan, 'n éisd do chluas
Ri creutair truagh a rinn do làmh,
Ag éigheach,—*Athair*! gabh dhiom truas,
'S leig fuarach do ghoil smear mo chnamh?

"Eisd o mo Dhia! mo thagradh bochd,
'S gach osna ghoirt 'ta teachd o m' chliabh,
'S aon athchuinge nis' iarram ort,
An deigh gach lochd a rinn mi riamh:

" 'Nuair ghuileas mi deich mìle bliadhn',
Sa'n lasair dhian so féin ga m' chràdh,
'Nuair sgìth'cheas deamhain' bhi'ga m' phian,
O deònaich 'Dhia gu'm faigh mi bàs!

" Ge truagh mo ghuidhe cha'n éisdear è
'Us fois no fè cha'n f haigh mi chaoidh
Ach beath' neo-bhàsmhor teachd as ùr
Gu'm neartach' ghiùlan tuille claoidh."

Ach stad mo rànn is pill air d'ais
O shloc na casgraidh dhéin a nios,
'Us féuch cionnas a bheir thu seòl',
Do'n dream tha beò nach d'théid iad sìos

A leughadair a'bheil e fìor,
Na chuir mi cheana sìos am dhàn?
Ma se 's gu'm bheil, thig 's lùb do ghlùn
Le ùrnuigh 's aithreachas gun dàil:

A dh ionnsuidh Iosa tcich gu luath,
A gabhail gràin 'us fuath do d' pheac',
Le creideamh fìor thoir ùmhlachd Dhà,
An' uil' àitheanta naomh a reachd.

Gabh Ris 'na oifigibh gu léir,
'S ri h-aon diu na cuir féin do chul;
Mar Fhàidh, mar Shagart' 'us mar Rìgh,
Chum slàinte, dìdean agus iùl.

Biodh eisempleir am beachd do shùl,
Chum d' uile ghluasad 'stiùr' d'a réir,
'S gach meadhon dh' òrduich E chum slàint
Bi féin g'an gnàthachadh gu léir.

As 'fhìreantachd dean bun amhàin.
'S na taic gu bràth ri d' thoilteanas féin :
'S ma 's àill leat éifeachd bhi 'na ghràs,
Na h-altrum peacadh dàimh a'd' chré.

Mar sin ged robh do chionta mòr,
Chum glòir do Tighearn' saorar thù,
'Us chum do shonais shiorruidh féin,
Air feadh gach ré a' seinn a chliù.

AM BRUADAR.

AIR bhith dhomhsa ann mo shuain
A' bruadar diomhain mar tha càch,

'Bhi' glacadh sonais o gach nì;
'Us è ga m' dhìbreadh ann's gach àit.

Air leam gu'n d'thainig neach a'm' chòir,
'S gu'n d'thuirt e rium, "Gur gòrach mi,
Bhi smuaintcach greim a ghlei'dh do'n ghaoith
No gu'n lion an saogh'l mo chrì'.

"Is diamhain dut bhi 'g iarraidh sàimh,
'N aon ni' no'n àit' air bith fo 'n ghréin;
Cha chlos do d' chorp an taobh so'n uaigh.
No d' anam 'n taobh so shuaimhneas Dé.

"An tra dh'ith Adhamh 'meas an tùs,
Am peacadh dhrùigh e air gach nì:
Lion e na h-uile ni le saothair,
'Us dh'fhàg e 'n saogh'l na bhriste crì'.

"Air sonas 'anama chaill e còir;
Mar ris gach sòlas bh' ànns a ghàr';
O sin ta 'shliochd nan deoiribh truagh;
Mar uain a mearachd air a' màthair.

"Ri mòilich chruaidh taid ruith gach nì,
'An duil gu 'm faigh an inntinn clos:
Ach dhoibh ta 'n saogh'l gun iochd no truas,
Mar mhuime choimheach fhuar gun tlus.

"Mar sin tha iad gun fhois no tàmh,
Ga 'n sàrach' glacadh faileas bréig;

'S a' deothal toil-inntinn o gach nì,
'Us iad mar chìochan seasg 'nam bèul.

" Bidh teanndachd éigin ort am feasd,
'S do dhòchas faicinn fuasgladh d'fhéum,
An còmhnuidh dhut mar fhad do làimh;
Ach gu bràth cha'n fhaigh dheth gréim.

" Chateagaisg d'fheuchainn's dearbhadh thù,
O dhùil 'us earbsa chuir sa' bhréig,
A rinn do mhealladh mìle uair.
S co fhada uat an diugh 's an dé.

" An ni bu mhò da'n d'thug thu miann,
Nach d'fhag a mhealtuinn riamh e searbh ?
Tha tuilleadh sonais ann an dùil,
Na th'ann an crùn le bhi na shealbh.

" Ceart mar an ròs a ta sa' ghàrr',
Seargaidh a bhlàth 'nuair théid a bhuain
Mu'n gann a ghlacas tu e d'làimh,
Tréigidh fhàile e 's a shnuadh.

" Ni 'bheil aon neach o thrioblaid saor,
Am measg a' chinne daoin' air fad.
'S co lionmhor osna th'aig an rìgh,
'Us th'aig an neach is ìsle staid.

" Tha 'smùdan féin a ceann gach fóid
'Us dòruinn ceangailt' ris gach maith ;

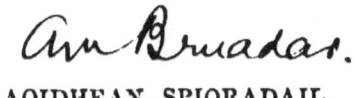

Tha'n ròs a' fàs air drisibh géur.
'S an taic' a chéil' tha mhil 's an gath.

" Ged chì thu neach 'an saibhreas mòr
Na meas a shòlas bhi thar chach :
An tobar 's glaine chì do shùil,
Tha ghrùid 'na ìochdar gabhail tàmh :

" 'S mu chuireas d'anail e 'na ghluas,
Le tarruing chabhaig suas a'd' bhéul,
Dùisgidh an ruadhan dearg a nìos,
'S le gaineamh lìonaidh e do dhéud.

" 'S ged chì thu neach 'an inbhe àrd,
Tha e mar nead am bàrr na craoibh ;
Gach stoirm a bagra' thilgeadh nuas,
'Us e air luasgadh leis gach gaoith.

" An neach is fearr tha 'n saogh'l a' riar'.
Tha fiaradh éigin ann 'na staid,
Nach dean a sheòltachd 'us a strì.
Am feasd a dhìreachadh air fad.

" Mar bhata fiar an aghaidh chéil,
A ta o shuidheach' féin do-chur ;
A réir mar dhìreas tu a bharr,
'S co cinnteach ni thu cam a bhun.

" Na h-Iudhaich' thionail beag no mòr,
De'n Mhana dhòirteadh orra 'nuas ;

H

'Nuair chuir gach neach a chuid 'sa chlàr,
Cha robh air bàrr no dadum uaith :

" Mar sin a ta gach sonas saogh'lt,
A ta thu faotainn ann a' d' làimh,
Fa chomhair saibhreas, 's inbhe cùirt
Tha caitheamh, cùram, agus cràdh.

" Ged chàrn thu òr a' d' shlige suas
Fa chomhair fàsaidh 'n luaidh da réir
'Us ge do chuir thu innte rìogh'chd
A mheidh cha dìrich i'na dhéigh.

" Tha cuibhrionn iomchuidh aig gach neach
'S ged tha thu meas gur tuille b' f hearr :
Cha d'thoir an t-anabharr th'ann an sud,
Am feasd an cudthrom as a chràdh.

" O iomluas d' inntinn tha do phian ;
A' diùlta 'n diugh na dh'iarr thu 'n dé :
Cha chomasach an saogh'l do riar',
Le d' anamianna 'n aghaidh chéil'.

" Na 'm faigheadh toil na feòl' a rùn,
D'a mianna bruideil dh'iarradh sàth ;
Flaitheas a b' àird cha'n iarradh ì,
Na annta sud bhi sìorruidh 'snàmh.

" Ach ged a b' ionmhuinn leis an f heòil.
Air talamh còmhnachadh gach ré :

Bhiodh dùrachd d' ardain agus d' uaill,
Cho arda shuas ri Cathair Dhé,

" Ach nam b' àill leat sonas buan,
Do shlighe thabhair suas do Dhia,
Le dùrachd, creideamh, agus gràdh,
'Us sàsaichidh E d' uile mhiann.

" Tha 'n cuideachd sud gach ni san t-saogh'l,
Tha 'n comas dhaoine shealbhach' fior ;
Biadh, agus aodach, agus slàint,
'Us saorsa, càirdeas, agus, sìth."

An sin do mhosgail as mo shuain,
'Us dh'fhag mo Bhruadar mi air fad :
'Us leig mi dhiom bhi ruith gach sgàil,
'Us dh'fhàs mi toilichte le m' staid.

———

AN GAISGEACH.

CHA bu ghaisgeach Alasdair mòr,
  No Cesar thug an Ròimh gu géill ;
Oir, ged a thug iad buaidh air càch,
  Dh' fhan iad 'nan tràill' d'amiannaibh féin.

Cha ghaisg' an ni bhi liodairt dhaoin',
  'S cha chliù bhi ann an caonnaig tric :

Cha 'n uaisle inntinn àrdan borb,
  'S cha treubhantas bhi garg gun iochd,

Ach 's gaisgeach esan a bheir buaidh
  Air eagal beatha, 's uamhunn bàis,
'Sa chòmh'laicheas le misnich crì',
  Na h-uile ni a ta dha 'n dàn.

Le gealtachd ciont, cha teich air cùl
  'S an àm san dùisg a choguis féin,
A tagradh, éisdidh e gu ciùin.
  'S an ceartas dùinidh e a béul,

'S e 'n gaisgeach èsan 'bheir fo' chìs,
  A thoil chum strìochd' do reusan ceart,
'S a smuaintean ceannairceach gu léir,
  Bhi 'n òrdugh géilleachdainn d'a smachd.

A mhianna brùideil saltraidh sìos,
  'S mar bhuill a chuirp fo' chìs a'taid,
S cha'n irislich e féin gu'n riar,
  O nach gu riaghladh rugadh iad.

San òidhch 'nuair luidheas è chum suain,
  Bi'dh shubhailcean mu'n cuairt da féin,
Mar shaighdearan mu thiomchioll rìgh,
  'Ga dhìdean o gach nàmhaid tréun.

'Sa mhaduinn 'nuair a dh'eireas suas,
  Cruinnichidh smuaintean as gach àit,

'S e féin 'na 'n ceann mar chaiptean scòlt',
   Ga'n suidheachadh 'an òrdugh blàir.

Chum cogadh 'n aghaidh miann na feòl',
   Gach bochdainn, 's dòruinn 'ta san t-saogh'l
Gach ribe 'us gach innleachd bàis,
   Ta 'n deamhan 'gnàthach' 'n aghaidh dhaoin'

Tha inntinn daingeann mar a' chreag,
   Cha charaich eagal e no fiamh:
Ta shùilean furachair 'us géur,
   'Us léir dha 'n dubhan cróm troi 'n bhiadh.

Gu diomhain nochdaidh 'n saogh'l a ghlòir,
   Gach òr 'us inbhe mhòr a t'ann;
Ta saibhreas aig' cho pailt 'na chrì',
   'S gur truagh leis rìgh is crùn mu cheann.

'Us ge do sgaoil an strìopach lìon,
   Gu ghlàc' le innleachdaibh a mais';
Cha drùidh air dealanach a sùl,
   'S cha leagh i 'rùn le 'miannaibh laist'.

A nàmh cha choisinn air gu bràth,
   Ged fhaigh e sàrachadh rè uair;
'S e 'neart 's a shlàinte cridhe brùit,
   'Us air a ghlùinibh bheir e buaidh.

'S i 'n fhìrinn ghlan is clogaid dà,
   'Us gràs a' chreideamh aig' mar sgiath;

'S e'n sgriobtuir naomh a chlaidheamh géur
   'S a mhisneach ta gu léir 'an Dia.

Tha sìothchaint aig 'na inntinn féin,
   'S a choguis réidh ris anns gach nì:
Ta saibhreas aig' nach léir do dhaoin,
   'Us air nach cuir an saoghal crìoch.

Ri miodal tlà cha 'n éisd a chluas,
   'Us sgainneal grannd cha bhuair a shìth
Cha ghabh e eagal á droch-sgéul,
   'Us tuaileas bréig cha lot a chrì'.

O m' anam! dùisg 'us deasaich d' airm,
   'S gabh fàrmad ris a' ghaisgeach thréun,
'Us d' anamianna cuir fo' chìs,
   Chum rìogh'chd a cheannsach' annad féin.

Biodh d' inntinn ard osceann nan spéur,
   Cha 'n 'eil fo 'n ghréin ach pòrsan truagh;
Mar tholman ùire faic an saogh'l,
   'Us daoin' mar sheangain air mu'n cuairt.

A null 'sa nall gun fhois gun tàmh
   A' cruinneach' as gach àit do'n cist'
Gu lìonmhor marcachd thar a chéil'
   'S a' trod gu géur mu bhioran brist'.

'Nuair chì thu 'n sealladh so de'n t-sluagh
   Do smuainte cruinnich suas gu léir,

A shealbhach' saibhreas, sonas, 's sìth,
Air nach tig crìoch a' d' anam féin.

———

AN CLAIGEANN.

'S mi 'm shuidh aig an uaigh,
Ag amharc mu bruaich,
Feuch Claigeann gun snuagh air làr:
Do thog mi e suas,
A' tiomach' gu truagh,
Ga' thionndadh mu 'n cuairt am làimh.

. Gun àille gun dreach,
Gun aithne gun bheachd;
Air duine theid seach 'na dhàil
Gun fhiacail 'na dhéud,
No teanga 'na bhéul,
No slugan a ghleusas càil.

Gun rughadh 'na ghruaidh
'S e rùisgte gun ghruaig;
Gun èisdeachd 'na chluais do m' dhàn
Gun anail 'na shròin,
No àile de'n fhòd,
Ach lag far 'm bu chòir bhi àrd.

Gun dealradh 'na shùil,
No rosg uimpe dùn',

No fradharc ri h-iùl mar b' àbh'sd.
    Ach durragan cróm,
    A chleachd bhi san tóm,
Air cladhach' dà tholl 'nan àit.

    Tha 'n eanchainn bha 'd chùl,
    Air tionndadh gu smùr,
Gun tionnsgal no sùrd air d'f hèum :
    Gun smuainteach' a'd' dhàil,
    Mu philleadh gu bràth,
A chearteach'. na dh'fhàg thu a' d' dhéidh.

    Cha 'n innis do ghnùis,
    A nise co thu,
Ma's rìgh no ma's diùc thu féin
    S' ionann Alasdair mòr,
    'Us tràill a dhìth lòin.
A dh' éug air an òtrach bhréun.

    Fhir dheanamh, na h-uaigh'
    Nach cagair thu 'm chluais,
Co 'n claigeann so fhuair mi 'm làimh?
    'S gu 'n cuirinn ris ceisd,
    Mu ghnàths mu 'n do theasd ;*
Ge d' nach freagair e' m' feasd mo dhàn.

    'M bu mhaighdeann deas thu,
    Bha sgiamhàch a' d' ghnùis,

---

* Mu'n D'eug e.

'S deagh shuidheach' a' d' shùil da réir?
Le d' mhaise mar lìon,
A ribeadh mu chrì',
Gach òganaich chì thu féin.

Tha nise gach àgh,
Bha cosnadh dhut gràidh,
Air tionndadh gu gràin gach neach ;
Marbhaisg air an uaigh,
A chreach thu de n' bhuaidh,
Bha ceangailt' ri snuadh do dhreach.

No 'm breitheamh ceart thù,
Le tuigs' agus iùl,
Bha réiteach gach cùis do'n t-sluagh ;
Gun aomadh le pàirt',
Ach dìteadh gu bàs,
Na h-eucoir bha dàicheil cruaidh ?

No 'n do reic thu a chòir,
Air ghlacaid de'n òr,
O 'n dream da 'n robh stòras pailt?
'Us bochdan an t-sluaigh.
Fo fhoirneart ro chruaidh,
A' fulang le cruas na h-airc.

'S mar robh thusa fior,
Ann a d' oifig am binn.
'S gun d'rinn thu an dìreach fiar ;

'S co cinnteach an nì,
Nuair thainig do chrìoch,
Gu 'n deachaidh do dhìt' le Dia.

Léigh.   No 'n robh thu a d' léigh,
A' leigheas nan créuchd,
'S a deanamh gach eugail slàn?
A' d'ìoc-shlaintibh mòr,
A' deanamh do bhòsd,
Gu 'n dìbreadh tu chòir o'n bhàs?

Mo thruaighe gu'n thréig,
Do leigheas thu féin,
'Nuair bha thu fo eucail chruaidh:
Gun fhoghnadh gun stà,
Am purgaid no 'm plàsd,
Gu d' chumail aon trà o'n uaigh.

malair.   No 'n seanalair thù,
A choisinn mor-chliù
Le d' shèoltachd a stiùradh airm?
Air naimhde toirt buaidh,
Ga 'n cur anns an ruaig,
'S ga 'm fàgail nan cruachaibh marbh:

'N robh do chlaidheamh gun bheairt,
No 'n d' fhág thu do neart,
'Nuair choinnich thu feachd na h-uaigh.
'Nuair b' éigin dut géill,

A dh'aindeoin do dhéud,
A dh' armailt' do bhéistibh truagh?

Tha na durraig gu tréun,
Ri d' choluinn' cur séisd,
'S a' cosnadh ort féisd gach là;
'Us claigeann do chinn,
'Na ghearasdan dion,
Aig daolagan dìblidh 'n tàmh:

Cuid a' claodhach' do dhéud.
A steach ann do bhéul,
S cuid eile a' réub do chluas;
Cuid eile nan sgùd,
Tigh'nn a mach air do shùil,
A spùinneadh 'sa rùsg' do ghruaidh.

No m' fear thu bha pòit,   *misgeadair.*
Gu tric san taigh-òsd,
'S tu cridheil ag òl nan dram?
Nach iarradh dhut féin,
Do fhlaitheanas Dhé,
Ach beirm a bhi 'g éiridh' d' cheann?

Nach iarradh tu 'cheòl,
Ach mionnan mu'n bhòrd,
'Us feuchainn co 'n dòrn bu chruaidh
Mar bhò no mar each,

Gun tuigse gun bheachd,
S tu brùchdadh 'sa sgeith mu'n chuaich?

Na 'n duin' thu bha gluas'd
Gu ceanalta, suairc,
Gu measara, stuam, mu d' bhòrd;
Le miannaibh do chré,
Fo' chuibhrichean géur,
'N am suidhe gu féisd 's gu sògh?

No' n geocaire mòr,
Bha gionach air lòn,
Mar choin ann am feòlach dhearg;
A' toileach' do mhiann,
Bha duilich a riar,
'S tu géilleadh mar dhia do d' bholg?

Tha nise do bhrù,
Da 'n robh thu a' lùb',
De ghaineamh 'us ùir glè làn
'S do dheudach air glas',
Mu d' theangaidh gun bhlas,
Fo' gheimhlichean prais a' bhàis.

No 'm morair ro mhòr,
A thachair am dhòrn,
Neach aig an robh còir air tìr;
Bha iochdmhor ri bochd,

A' cluthach' nan nochd,
'Réir pailteas a thoic 's a ni?

No 'n robh thu ro chruaidh,
A' feannadh do thuath,
'S a tanach' an gruaidh' le màl;
Le agartas géur
A glacadh an spréidh
'S am bochdainn ag éighcach dáil?

Gun chridh' aig na daoin',
A bh'air lomadh le h-aois,
Le 'n claigeannaibh maola truagh;
Bhi seasamh a' d' chòir,
Gun bhoineid 'nan dòrn,
Ge d' tholladh gaoth reòt' an cluas.

Tha nise do thràill,
Gun urram a' d' dhàil,
Gun ghearsom, gun mhàl gun mhòd;
Mor mholadh do'n bhàs,
A chasgair thu trà,
'S nach d' fhuiling do stràic fo'n fhòd.

No 'm ministear thù,
Bha tagra' gu dlù,
Ri pobull 'an ùghdarras Dé;
Ga 'm pilleadh air ais,

Bha 'g imeachd gu bras,
Gu h-ifrinn na casgraidh dhéin?

No 'n robh thu gun sgoinn,
Mar mhuime mu chloinn,
Gun chùram de dh'oighreachd Dhé;
Na 'm faigheadh tu 'n rùsg.
Bha coma co dhiù,
Mu'n t-sionnach bhi stiùradh an tréud;

Leam 's cinnteach gu'n d'fhuair,
Do dheanadas duais,
'Nuair rainig thu 'm Buachaill' mòr:
'Nuair chuartaich am bàs,
A steach thu 'na laith'r,
Thoirt cunntas a' d' thàlann dò.

No 'n ceann thu bha làn,
De dh' innleachdan bàis.
Gu seòlta ga 'n tàth'dh r' a chéil;
Ga'n cur ann an gniomh,
Gun umhail gun fhiamh,
A freagra' do Dhia 'nan dèigh?

'N robh tcanga nam bréug,
Gun chuibhreach fo d' dhéud.
A' togail droch sgeil air càch;
Gath puinnsein do bhéil.

An claigeann.

Mar naithir a' téum,
Sa' lotadh nan céud gach là?

Tha i nise 'na tàmh,
Fo' cheangal a bhàis,
Gun sgainneal o phlàigh na dùch'.
'Us durragan grànnd,
Air lobhadh 'na h-àit,
An déigh dhoibh a cnàmh gu cul.

'S mu lean thu do ghnàths,
Gu leabaidh do bhàis,
Gun tionndadh' na thrà ri còir;
Car tamuill na h-uair',
Dean flaitheas de'n uaigh,
Gus an gairmear thu suas gu mòd:

Mar losgann dubh grànnd,
Ag iomairt a' smàg,
Gu 'n éirich thu 'n aird o'n t-sloc;
Thoirt coinneamh do Chrìosd,
'Na thigheachd a rìsd,
A dh' fhaotainn làn diol a'd' olc.

'Nuair théid thu f'a bhinn,
Ni cheartas do dhìt';
Ga d' fhògradh gu sìorruidh uaith,
Gu lasair gu d' phian',

Chaidh a dheasach' do'n Diabh'l,
Sa mhallachd gu dian 'ga d' ruag'.

'N sin cruaidhichidh Dia
Do chnaimhean mar iar'n.
'Us d' fheithean mar iallaibh prais;
'Us teannaichidh d' fheòil,
Mar innein nan òrd,
Nach cnàmh i le mòid an teas.

No 'n ceann thu 'n robh ciall,
'Us còlas air Dia,
'S gun d' rinn thu a riar 'sa chòir:
Ged tha thu 'n diugh rùisgt',
Gun aithne', gun iùl,
Gun teanga', gun sùil, gun sròin.

Gabh misneach san uaigh,
Oir éiridh tu suas,
'Nuair chluinneas tu fuaim an stuic,
'S do thruailleachd gu léir,
Shìos fàgaidh tu d' dhéigh,
Aig durragan bréun an t-sluic.

'N sin deasaichidh Dia,
Do mhaise mar' ghrian,
Tha 'g éiridh o sgiath nam' beann
'Cur fradharc ro ghéur,

'S na suilean so féin,
'S iad a' dealradh mar réulta a'd' cheann.

Do theanga 's do chàil,
    Ni ghleusadh gun dàil,
A chantuinn 'na àros cliù:
    'Us fosglaidh do chluas,
    A dh'éisteachd ri fuaim,
A mholaidh th' aig sluagh a' chùirt.

'Nuair dhealraicheas Criosd,
    Na thigheachd a rìs,
A chruinneach' nam fìrean suas:
    'N sin bheir thu do léum,
    Thoirt coinneamh dha féin,
Mar iolair nan spéur aig luaths.

'Nuair dh'eireas tu 'n àird,
    Grad chuiridh ort fàilt.
A mhealtuinn a chàirdeas féin,
    Gun dealach' gu bràth,
    R'a chomunn no ghràdh,
A steach ann am Fàrras Dé.

Fhir 'chluinneas mo Dhàn,
    Dean aithreachas trà,
'M feadh a mhaireas do shlaint 's do bheachd;
    Mu'n d'thig ort am bàs
    Nach leig thu gu bràth,
Air geata nan gràs a steach.

I

AN GEAMHRADH.

Do theirig an sàmhradh.
   'S tha'n geamhradh teachd dlù oirn,
Fior nàmhaid na chinneas,
   Teachd a mhilleadh ar dùcha:
Ga saltairt fo' chasaibh,
   'S d'a maise 'ga rùsgadh;
Gun iochd ann ri dadum,
   Ach a sladadh 's a plùnndrainn.

Sgaoil oirnne a sgiathan,
   'S chuir e ghrian air a chùlthaobh
As an nead thug e'n t-àlach,
   Neo-bhàigheil g'ar sgiùrsadh:
Sneachd iteagach gle gheal,
   O na speuraibh teachd dlù oirn',
Clacha-meallain 's gaoth thuathach,
   Mar luaidhe 'us mar fhùdar.

'Nuair shéideas e anàll,
   Cha 'n fhag anam am flùran;
Tha 'bhilean mar shiosar,
   Lomadh lios de gach ùr-ros:
Cha bhi sgeudach air coille,
   No doire nach rùisg e;
No sruthan nach tachd e,
   Fo leacannan dù'-ghorm.

Fead reòta a chléibhe,
  Tha séideadh na doinionn,
A chuir beirm anns an fhàirge,
  'S a dh' at' garbh i na tonnan ;
S a bhinntich an clàmhuinn,
  Air airde gach monaidh,
'S ghlan sgùr e na réultan,
  D' ar péile le'n solus.

Tha gach beathach 'us duine,
  Nach d' ullaich 'na shéason,
Ga 'n sgiùrsa' le gaillionn
  Gun talla' gun éudach : '
'S an dream a bha gniomhach,
  'Fàs iargalt' mi-dhéirceil :
Nach d' thoir iasachd do'n leisgean,
  Anns an t-sneachda ge d' éug e.

Tha 'n seillean 's an seangan,
  A bha tional an stòrais,
Le gliocas gun mhearachd,
  A'toirt aire do'n dòruinn :
'G ithe bidh 's ag òl meala,
  Gun ghainne air lòn ac',
Fo' dhion anns an talamh.
  O anail an reòta.

Tha na cuileagan ciatach,
  'Bha diomhain san t-sàmhradh,

'S na gathanaibh gréine,
     Gu h-éibhinn a dannsa;
Gun deasach 'gun chùram,
     Roi' dhuldachd a gheamhraidh:
Tha iad' nise a' bàsach',
     Anns gach àite le teanntachd,

Ach éisd rium a shean-duin'.
     S' tuig an samhladh tha 'm stòri',
Tha 'm bàs a' teachd teann ort,
     Sud an geamhradh tha 'm òran:
'S ma gheibh e thu d' leisgein,
     Gun deasach' fa' chòmhail,
Cha dean aithreachas crìche,
     Do dhìonadh o'n dòrainn.

Gur mithidh fàs diadhaidh,
     'S do chiabhan air glasadh,
'Na bearnaibh do dhéudach,
     'Us d' eudan air casadh;
Do bhathais air rùsgadh,
     'S do shùilean air prabadh,
Agus croit ort air lùbadh,
     Chum na h-ùire do leaba'.

Tha na sruthanan cráobhach,
     'Bha sgaoilcadh a' d' bhallaibh
Gu mireagach, buailteach,
     Clis, gluasadach, tana;

A nise air traoghadh
  O 'n taomachadh thairis,
O'n a ragaich 'sa dh' fhuaraich
  Teas uabhar na fala.

Balg séididh na beatha,
  Tha air caitheamh gun fhéum ann.
'S o chrup ann ad' chliabh e,
  Gur e 'm pian' bhi 'ga shéideadh:
Tha 'n corp a chruit chiùil ud,
  Air diùltadh dhut gléusadh;
'S comhar' cinnt' air a thasgaidh,
  Bhi lasach' a théudan.

Theich maduinn na h-òige,
  'Us treòir mheadhon latha
Tha 'm feasgar air ciaradh,
  'S tha ghrian ort a' laidhe:
'S mu bha thusa diomhain,
  Gun ghniomh 'us gun mhaitheas;
Gu h-ealamh bi d' dhùsgadh,
  Mu'n dùinear ort flaitheas.

'Réir caithe na beatha,
  'S tric leatha gun crìoch i;
Bidh an cleachda' fàs làidir,
  Do-fhàsach o'n ìnntinn:
Na labhair an scan-fhocal,
  'S deimhin leam fìor e,

" An car théid san t-sean-mhaid'
  Gur h-ainmic leis dìreadh."

Ach òganaich thréibhich
  Thoirs' éisdeachd do m' òran,
'S leig dhiot bhi mi-chéillidh,
  Ann an céitean na h-òige
Tha aois agus éaslaint,
  Air do dheigh ann an tòir ort;
'S mu ni h-aon aca gréim ort,
  Pillidh d' aoibhneas gu bròn dut.

An aois a ta 'n tòir ort,
  Bheir i leòn ort nach saoil thu;
Air do shùilibh bheir ceathach,
  'Us treabhaidh i d' aodan:
Bheir i crith-reo'dh mu d' ghruaig',
  'Us neul uaine an aoig leis,
'S cha d'thig aiteamh na grian ort,
  'Bheir an liath-reo'dh a chaoidh' dhiot.

Bheir na's measa na sud ort,
  Fàilinn tuigs' agus réusain;
Dìth leirsinn a' d' inntinn;
  · Dìth cùimhn' agus géire;
Dìth gliocais chum gnothaich;
  Dìth mothaich a'd' chéudfadh:
'S gu'm fàs thu mar leanabh,
  Dhìth spionnaidh 'us céille.

Fàsaidh 'n cridhe neo-aithreach,
  'S neo ealamh chum tionndadh,
Aon tagra' cha drùigh air,
  'S cha lùb e d'a ionnsuidh:
Ceart mar tha 'n talamh,
  'N am gaillinn 'us teanntachd;
Ged robh milltean 'dol thairis,
  Cha dean aile sa' chàbhsair.

Faic séason na bliadhna,
  'S dean ciall uath a tharuing:
S ma's àill leat gu'm buain thu,
  Dean rùdhar 'san earrach;
Dean connadh san t-sàmhradh,
  Ni sa' gheamhradh do gharadh;
'S ma dhìbreas tu 'n séason,
  Dhut 's éigin bhi falamh.

'S mar cuir thu sìol fallain,
  Ann an earrach, na h-òige,
Cho chinnteach 's am bàs dut,
  Cuiridh Sàtan droch phòr ann:
A dh' fhàsas 'na dhubhaile,
  'S 'na luibheannan feòlmhor:
S bi'dh do bhuain mar a chuir thu,
  Ma's subhaile no do-bheart,

Ma bhios d' òige gun riaghladh,
  'S d' ana-miannan gun taod riu,

Gum fàs iad cho fiadhaich,
  'S nach srian thu ri d' aois iad :
Am meangan nach sniomh thu,
  Cha spion thu 'na chraoibh e ;
Mar shìneas e ghéugan,
  Bidh a fhréumhan a' sgaoileadh.

Tha do bheatha neo-chinnteach
  O 'n teinn a bheir bàs ort,
Uime sin bi ri dìchioll
  Do shìth dheanamh tràthail :
'S e milleadh gach cùise
  Bhi gun chùram 'cur dàil innt' ;
S ionann aithreachas crìche,
  'S bhi cur sìl mu Fheill-Màrtuinn.

Tha ghrian anns na spéuraibh
  A' ruith réise gach latha ;
'S i giorrach' do shaoghail,
  Gach òidhche a luidheas ;
'S dlù ruitheas an spàla,
  Troi' shnath'naibh do bheatha :
Tha' fitheadh dhut léine,
  'Ni béisdean a chaitheamh.

'S ma ghoideas e dlù ort,
  Gun do dhùil bhi r'a thighinn ;
'N sin fosglaidh do shùilean,
  'S chì thu' chùis thar a mithich ;

'Bidh do choguis 'ga d' phianadh,
  Mar sgian ann do chridhe ;
'S co-ionann a giùlan,
  'S luidhe rùisgt' ann an sgitheach.

Faic a' chuileag 'ga dìteadh
  Le sìonntaibh an nàduir,
'S o dhìbir i 'n séason,
  Gur h-eigin di bàsach' :
Faic gliocas an t-seangain,
  Na thional cho tràthail,
'S dean cisempleir leanail,
  Chum d' anam a' shàbhal'.

URNAIGH.

O! Thighearn' 'us a Dhia na glòir,
  An t-Ard-Righ mòr os-ceann gach sluaigh,
Cia dàna ni air d' ainm ro mhòr
  Le bilibh neò-ghlan a bhi luaidh !

Na h-aingle 's airde rinneadh leat,
  Cia lag an neart ; 's cia dall an iùl !
Cia aineolach air d' oibre mòr !
  'S cia goirid air do ghlòir an cliù !

Am beachd do shùilean fiorghlan féin,
   Cha 'n eil na réultan 's airde glan :
'S cha 'n 'eil na h-aingle 's naomha 'n glòir,
   'An làthair do Mhorachd-sa gun smal.

Ach O an dean thu d' isleach' féin,
   A dh'éisdeachd cnuimhe anns an ùir !
Fo' stòl do chos a' gabhail tàmh,
   'S nach faic ach sgàile beag do d' ghnuis

Na lasadh d' fhearg O Dha nan dùl,
   Am feadh a dheanam ùrnuigh riut :
'S mo pheacadh aidicheam le nàir,
   'S an truailleachd ghràineil anns' na thuit.

Mo chiont tha mar na sléibhte mòr :
   'Us leòn iad mi le iomadh lot :
Ta m' anam bochd le 'n cudthrom brùit,
   'S o m' shùilibh' fàsg' nan déura goirt.

An comas dut a Dhia nam feart,
   Mo shaor' gun cheartas chur air cùl !
'S mu shaorar le do thròcair mì
   'M bheil neach san t-saogh'l a dhìteas tù !

Nach éigin dut mo sgrios gu bràth,
   Mur àicheadh thu do cheartas géur !
Le m' chionta oillteil, 's gann a dh' fhàg
   Mi iochd, no gràs, a' d' roghainn féin.

Urnaigh

Gach uile mhallachd ata sgrìobht'
. A'd' fhocal fior le bagra' teann,
O Thighearn thoill mi aig do làimh,
    Gum biodh iad càrnaicht' air mo cheann.

Ge d' fhàs na neamhan dubh le gruaim,
    'S mo bhual' le tairneanaich do neart;
Ge d' thilg thu mi gu ifrinn shìos,
    Gu sìorruidh aidicheam do cheart.

Gidheadh am faod an lasair thréun
    A sgoilteas as a chéil an tuil;
Drùghadh orm troi' ùmhlachd Chrìosd,
    'S mi 'gabhail dìon a steach fo' fhuil?

An fhuil a dhiol do cheartas teann,
    'S a dhoirteadh air a chrann gu làr,
'S ann aisd' tha m' earbsa, O mo Rìgh !
    Nach dìt thu m'anam air a sgàth.

Dean m' ionnlad glan, O Dhia na sìth !
    'S an tobar ioc-shlaint 'bhrùchd a thaobh:
A bheir dhomh beatha as a bhàs,
    'S o m' thruaillidheachd a ni mi saor.

Daingnich mo chreideamh ann 'na bhàs,
    'Us beothaich gràdh am chridhe stigh,
'Us neartaich mi chum umhlachd dha,
    'An uil' aitheanta naomh a lagh.

O dean mo phlanndach' ann an Crìosd !
   'S mo chrìonach brisidh mach le blàth ;
Is bi'dh gach subhailc 's naomha gléus,
   Mar mheas a' lùb mo ghéug gu làr.

Gach inbhe 'n cuir thu mi san t-saogh'l
   Dean daonnan toilicht' mi le m' staid ;
Ma's bochd, no beàrtach, tinn, no slàn,
   Do thoil gu bràth biodh deant' air fad.

O ! 's gràsmhor Dia 'nuair bheir e seach !
   'S gu beachd tha DIÙLTADH *làn de* GHRADH;
'S fior-bheannachd ann an atharach dreach;
   Gach CROIS *'us* CRÉACH *a thig o làimh.*

O buidheachas do Dhia nan gràs
   Chuir thugam Slanuighear nam buadh ;
Eirig mo shaorsa chì 'na bhàs ;
   'S an luach a phàidh' air m' anam truagh.

'S e féin a chlaon a dhruim fo 'n chuail ;
   Chum m'anam dhireadh suas gu Dia !
Chosd gach tiodhlac 'th' agam uaith,
   Geur chràdh 'us osna chruaidh d'a chliabh.

Mo smuaintean talmhaidh tog gu nèamh,
   'Us thoir dhomh earlas air do ghràdh,
A dh' fhògras m' eagal uile uam,
   'S a shaoras mi o uamhunn bàis.

'N sin atadh tonnan borb a' chuain,
   'Us beucadh torrunn chruaidh nanspéur;
Thigeadh crith-thalmhuinn gort, 'us plàigh,
   Bhios 'roinn a' bhàis gach taobh a théid.

Bi thus' a'd' Dhia do m'anam féin,
   'S bi'dh iad gu léir dhomh,'n càirdeas gràidh;
Cha loisg an tein' gun òrdugh uat,
   Cha sluig an cuan, 's cha sgrios a phlàigh;

Am feadh bhios cumhachd ann a d' làimh,
   Bidh mise sàbhailt'ò gach olc:
'S cha 'n eagal leam gu 'm bi mi 'n dìth,
   Gu sìorruidh no gu 'm fàs thu bochd.

Mo dhùrachd, m' eagal, 's m' uile mhiann
   A' m' Dhia tha còmh'lachadh gu léir;
Oir nèamh, 'us talamh, 's ifrinn shìos,
   A ta iad do mo Rìgh-s' a' géill'.

CRIOCH.

AN ENGLISH VERSION

OF

DUGALD BUCHANAN'S SPIRITUAL SONGS.

AN ENGLISH VERSION

OF

DUGALD BUCHANAN'S SPIRITUAL SONGS.

THE MAJESTY OF GOD.

CONTENTS :—God is incomprehensible to men or angels—He is self-exist-
ent—Unchangeable—Infinite—His power in creation and providence
—The thought of the infinite oppressive to reason—God's riches of
creation—These cannot fully reveal Him—His Word only can.

WHAT is God, or what His name, the highest angels
cannot comprehend. Hid He is in shining light,
which neither eye nor thought can penetrate. From
Himself His being flows. Uncreated are His attri-
butes. His nature infinite; and by Divine perfection all maintained. He was not young, nor old
shall be. From age to age He changes not. Nor
sun nor moon can mete His days; for they are all but
changing things. When grace or glory He reveals,
immortal day shines from His eye. Quickly the
hosts of heaven high, vail their faces with their
wings. If He reveals His face in wrath, terror per-
vades the firmament. At His rebuke the ocean flees,
and earth itself with terror quakes. The works of
nature grow and fade. From change to change

K

they ever go. In all His actions He is one, He neither ebbs nor flows. Angels and men to nothing are akin ; the womb from whence we all have sprung. But God's perfection high, eternal is, and from its very nature infinite.

When Nothing heard His mighty voice, creation great at once to being sprang—this globe with all its teeming fulness—the heavens on high with all their host. Then all His works He did survey, and bless'd each creature in its state. Of all His mighty works that He had done, not one did need to be improved. He guides the motion of the stars. On His hand's palm they all revolve. In the hollow of His hand creation is. On Him it leans, and is supported by His mighty arm.

Oh, God ! Thy being who compass can ! Reason is swallowed up in its attempts to fathom it. Both men and angels are in their attempts, as if they tried the ocean to contain within the compass of a little mussel shell.

From everlasting Thou art King. This world is a thing of yesterday. Of Thee how little have we heard ! But few Thy works beneath the Sun ! Though the Sun be turned into nothing, and all that in its light revolves; as little were they missed from among Thy wondrous works, as would the ocean miss a finger-drop.

In all its glory vast, creation cannot Thee reveal in all the fulness of Thy power. These wondrous works of Thine are but an earnest of Thy might. How vain for us of shallow reason to attempt to fathom what is infinite. The smallest letter of the

name of God too great a load for human reason is.
Of all the works, Thy mighty hand has made, none
can with Thee compare—nor any language 'mong the
sons of men, express Thy name, except Thy *Holy
Word* alone.

SUFFERINGS OF CHRIST.

CONTENTS :—The Incarnation the greatest wonder—Christ's birth—Persecution by Herod—His poverty—His miracles, and salvation—The
loaves and fishes multiplied—The storm stilled—The institution of
the Supper—Gethsemane—The treachery of Judas—The malice of
enemies—Calvary— Tis finished.

MY Saviour's sufferings my song recounts. How
greatly humbled was the King of kings in His lowly
birth, and in His ignominious death.   'Tis the greatest wonder ever told to men, the everlasting God became a sucking child.

When by the power of the Holy Ghost He was in
the Virgin's womb conceived, that He our human
nature might unite to His person all Divine.   His
Divinity was vailed.   The Word did flesh become.
The mystery of Godliness was then revealed in the
glorious person of the Son.

Born in a stable low.   A helpless orphan He.
None to tender kindly aid, nor friendly roof to shelter
Him from cold.   No royal retinue His person did at-
tend.   No royal robes had our Almighty King.
Horses and oxen all around the Lord, to whom all
glory bright is due.

Scarce was His advent known, when enemies great
arose.   He was forced to flee to Egypt land from

Herod the pursuing foe. This fierce avenger so intent to slay the Holy Lamb of God, issued malign behest to kill each babe throughout the land, hoping to slay the Saviour 'mong the rest.

Foxes have holes to cover them. Fowls have their nests on high. But He who made them all—the world and all its full, a wanderer was on earth, without a place of rest beneath the sun.

When He sojourned on earth 'mong men, to save. A Physician ever kind was He. A Physician skilled to heal. No malady His skill defied. By His word He healed them all. Tongues to the dumb He gave. Strength to the lame to walk. To deaf ones hearing gave. To the blind He gave their sight. The loathsome lepers He did cleanse. He made their bodies whole and sound. Diseases of the soul He healed ; and into life the dead restored.

The Gospel He did preach unto the poor. To captives bound in iron fetters and bondage sore, eternal liberty He did proclaim, if they the truth received by living faith—converted were, and all their carnal ways forsook.

Unto the barren wilderness with multitudes He goes. For days they listenèd to gracious heavenly words. Five thousand famishing were for lack of food. Very little bread had they. Of barley loaves they just had five. Of fishes, small, they just had two. This constituted all their store. On this little bread and fish, His blessing He pronounced. The food was multiplied. They all did eat. They all were satisfied with food, and did abundance leave behind. His blessing so increased their fare.

He stilled the stormy sea. Its raging billows

calmed. In His fist He compassed round the mighty hurricane. Who can the miracles recount—the wonders all that Jesus did. The world itself could not contain the register of all His mighty acts that He had done.

When the time was drawing nigh, that to glory He should go; He gathered His disciples and provided them a feast. Around a table furnished well with food, He seated them. Bread and wine were given them. Emblems of His flesh and blood. So to do as ordinance, to them He did command—to signify His sufferings great, which He endured for them, that eat and drink they ever should, the fruits of heavenly love, and to commemorate His death in generations yet to come.

When to Gethsemane He came. Behold His agonising pain. Behold the cup of wrath, that bitter cup so terrible to drink. Now is that cup put in His hand to take. See His pulse, how burns it in His holy frame. Bruised with the awful pressure—so sorely bruised, that bloody sweat exudes His raiment through, and falls in drops down to the ground. Behold Him kneeling down. Hear Him offering this resigning prayer : "Oh ! my beloved Father, if this with Thee accords. If possible it be, this cup, Oh ! let it pass from me. But for this end I came, my flock that I should save. Therefore, no favour shall I ask, but that Thy will for ever should be done. Oh ! 'twas an awful cup that now presented was. A world's sins pressing Him with all their dark desert. An eternity of punishment, of sufferings and pain, at once were laid upon the Son. This cup He had to drink.

By Satan, Judas see possessed. With devilish
duplicity his heart is filled. A crafty covetous
hypocrite that so disowned his God. A traitor to his
Saviour, his loving Master, and his Lord; betraying
Him to deadly foes. His dark design he seeks to
hide beneath the covering of a friendly kiss.

See Jesus, now a prisoner. No guilt in Him was
found. Behold Him stand in Pilate's court, that he
should Him condemn. He is condemned to die. The
judge unjust condemned the Christ. On testimony false
condemned. Reproached he was by his own conscience,
which witnessèd that innocent and true our Saviour
was. The Holy One they bind with cords—they
scourge—they beat with cruel blows. From off
His bones His flesh is torn. His holy body's
sorely bruised. Behold His gashing wounds. His
redeeming blood is shed for sin, a world to ransom,
quite unappreciated by men. Behold a crown of
prickly thorns by them is strongly plaited. To cover
Him with shame, and to increase His pain, compressed
they hard this crown upon His blessed brow. His head
is pierced with prickly thorns. With loathsome
filthy spittle mar they His face Divine. When thus
they placed upon his brow the shameful, painful
crown, with scarlet robe they clothed Him, and
mocking Him to scorn, put in His hand a royal reed,
with insult thus addressing Him—"Hail King of the
Jews!" And then they bend to Him the knee. With
violence, the Cross they Him compel to bear. Though
hard the task, that hour He yielded to their will.
Behold His strength is failing Him. His pulse is
ebbing fast. As He ascends the fatal mount He faints

beneath the cursed load. On the torturing couch behold Him stretched, a willing sacrifice for men. Behold Him stretched—denuded on the cross. His limbs disjointed. His holy body nailed into the tree—fast nailed with nails by hammer driven in. The cross they raise erect. Jesus is fixed thereon, hanging by the nails; enduring pain unutterable. Behold Him tortured in this posture—His wounds and sores enlargèd by His weight, as thus He is suspended. His precious holy blood falls fast upon the ground. Ignominious and painful is the death contrived for Him. But not a murmur uttered He. Nor did complaint escape against His cruel foes. He interceded for them. He interposed in their behalf: "Father forgive them, for they know not what they do." Behold Him sore distressed. The fierceness of the Father's wrath from every side on Him is poured. The Father's face of love is hid from Him. His light Divine is now withdrawn. The hour was dark, and in this painful state He thus exclaimed :—"My God, my God, why hast Thou thus forsaken me. Thy gracious face, Oh! hide thou not. Forsake me not in this my time of need." Mankind at large ; the hosts of angels high, not for a moment could endure the load of vengeance borne by Christ alone. It would at once destroy them all. The smallest measure of this fiery wrath would soon consume the world at large. At this solemn hour, the Lord of Hosts did summon round all reasonable beings ever made. By the cross He says to them, behold my love to men! Behold how sin I hate! See it in my fiery wrath—wrath poured out on my beloved Son. This of His sufferings the teaching is. Hear and perceive, ye sons of men, how dreadful 'tis to sin. In my sufferings see its meet reward. Behold the strictness of that justice, that laid hold of me for you. Not a farthing of the debt will it forego. My death alone can pay your debt to justice that you owe.

This death is accursed — painful — stinging— revengeful in every way—excruciating—ignominious —tedious beyond what words can tell. How dreadful, and how awful is the thought. Who can describe His woes. For six whole hours He hung alive, suspended by the sinews of His body, on that accursed tree. In the furnace of the wrath of God, His bodily strength fast ebbed away. As wax dissolves before the flame, so melted fast away His friendly loving heart. His tongue that guileless was—that ever plead His people's cause, fast cleaved unto His jaws. Those sufferings great, breaking—the thread of His most precious life. His vision pure, it fails. His eyes their wonted lustre lose. His trembling heart asunder cleaves. The noblest countenance that e'er was seen, assumes the palid hue of death. Methinks I see His face so pale, as thus the battle sore He fights. Methinks I see His wounds—His mangled flesh, torn by the cruel nails. The clotted blood I see. I see His strength abating fast. Methinks I see the ghastly look, as gathers it around. The beauty of the Lord I see departing fast. Methinks I hear His groans, and see the throbbings of His heart.

Now Jesus speaks. He said, " I greatly thirst." To Him they gave a drink of vinegar and gall.

Then said He, "It is finished." The work is now
fulfilled, I undertook to do. With mighty voice He
cried aloud. He bent His head, gave up the ghost,
and suffered pain no more. It was a startling cry.
Creation heard it! Rocks were rent. The dead—
they trembled in their graves. The Sun, in his
meridian brightness, darkened was. The hue of all
things changed. Creation seemed as if it would
expire. Heaven that ever joyous was—its hosts at
all times glad—their joy is changed to sadness.
Their heavenly music ceased. They saw their Maker
and their Lord, the Author of their being, lowly laid
in silent tomb, fast bound in death, He who planted
life in everything.

THE DAY OF JUDGMENT.

CONTENTS :—Careless state of the world—The Archangel sounds—The
dead arise—The righteous first—Then the wicked—The lost soul's ad-
dress to its body—The great of the earth rise—The devil appears—
The Judge descends—Description of Him and of a dissolving universe
— The Judge decides men's doom—Judas—Worldly men—Herod—
The books opened—Various classes of men described—The separation
—The righteous brought home—Their blessedness—The wicked driven
away—Their misery—Conclusion.

WHILE the majority of men love not Jesus nor His
cause. Nor yet believe that He shall come to judge
them by His holy laws. They slumber on in sinful
sleep. They dream of plenty of each thing. They
care not that when death shall come, they shall not
enter into Paradise—the Paradise of the King of
kings. In mercy by Thy word awaken them to see
their danger ere too late ; and bless my song to every
one that lends attentive ear thereto. Lord elevate

my earthly thoughts.   My tongue unlose to sing my
lay, that I may publish as I ought the dreadful glory
of the day of God.

At midnight hour when slumbering in deepest
sleep, the people quickly startled are, by sound of
God's great trumpet sounding high.   An archangel
then is seen, seated on a cloud, and with angelic
trumpet summons all the world, that they arise--that
quickly they arise and do appear before the judgment-
seat of God.   Oh ! listen all ye sons of men.   Now the
end of the world is come.   Spring to life, Oh all ye
dead, for truly Jesus now is come.   And at His mighty
trumpet blast, both seas and mountains quake with
fear.   The dead are startled in their graves.   The
living tremble as they hear.   And with His mighty
utterance, He earth asunder cleaves.   And like an
ant-hill moved when touched, the grave pours forth
its dead.   Each limb, each member—foot and hand,
that ever buried were in land or sea or battle-field,
shall come together.   Loud is the noise among the
bones, each coming to its place.   First the righteous
shall awake from long sepulchral rest.   Their souls
from glory shall descend to meet their bodies at the
grave.   With joy they lift their heads on high.
Their redemption now is come.   As tree adorned
with richest blossom, so they bloom, in image of their
risen Lord.   The Spirit's blessed work within, has
made them free from taint of sin ; and clothed with
righteousness of Christ, they shine in spotless purity.

The wicked thereafter rise.   They come like hateful monsters from their graves.   From hell their
miserable souls ascend to meet their bodies there.

And as the wretched weeping soul meets the hateful loathsome body, thus it speaks. Alas! Alas! why risen thou, to aggravate our double woe. Must I again return to thee as to a hateful loathsome prison. Must I again inhabit thee! Alas! Alas! that ever I a slave was to thy vile debasing lusts. Oh! shall I never from thee part; nor death at all dissolve the tie. Shall not the fire of hell consume thy bones; will not the wrath of God make end of thee—thy flesh consume—destroy?

Kings and mighty men arise. Shorn of all power, and of all rule, they are. They are not known among the multitude, from them that served as slaves. Haughty men—they that deigned not to submit themselves to God, behold them there upon their knees. To the mountains and the hills they pray. "Ye lofty mountains fall upon our heads. Pour upon us rocky showers. Consume us quite from off the land of those that living are, that we may never see the Lamb nor gaze upon His glory bright."

Then forth ascends the devil from his den of darkness, followed by his angels—hellish dusky train. Hard it is for him to do. But come he must dragging his chain behind—his prison fetters. Anon the firmament grows red as when the morning sun begins to dawn, diffusing fiery radiance—purple hue, announcing as his harbinger, that Jesus comes—that now is come the great, the dreadful day. Quickly the clouds asunder cleave—the chamber door by which goes forth the King of kings. The mighty Judge is now revealed in majesty and glory infinite. The rainbow circles round His head. His voice is as the sound of mighty torrents rushing through the vales. His glance as lightning flash, as bursts it through the intervening clouds. The sun, that brightest luminary, in the firmament supremely ruling, pales to the brightness of His glory. The infinite, ineffable effulgence shining from His face, outshines his light. The sun assumes a mourning dress. The moon is as if steeped in blood. The powers of heaven are shaken. The stars are shaken from their spheres. Tossed they are in airy space as fruit on pending bow, when tossed by mighty wind. They fall as drops, when heavy showers of rain descend. Their glory dies, as fades the lustre of the eye in death.

He sits on chariot of fire. Thunders peal around reverberating to the utmost confines of the heavens, tearing the clouds with violence terrific. From His chariot wheels there issues forth a stream of liquid fire. The flame in anger kindled is. The fiery flood pours forth on every side, and sets the world in universal flame. The elements are melted with the heat, as wax before the fire. Mountains and hills are in a blaze. The ocean boils. The stubborn mountains that refused to give their hidden stores—see them pouring forth. Behold the torrent of their melted treasures, which unsolicited they yield. Ye lovers, hoarders of your gold, by greed or wickedness or blood amassed. Your thirst now quench. Drink ye freely from this flood. Ye who made the world your stay, come. Its end lament. Behold its agonies. See how it wrestles as a strong man dying struggles in the grasp of death. Its pulse that erst

was fresh and cool—that beat so merrily 'mong hills,
through winding glen and valley ; now by the burning
heat is paralyzed.   Pervading its vast frame it drinks
its moisture up, turning it to airy vapour.   How
trembles it in every part and pore !   The rocks are
shaken !   They are moved from their foundations in
the everlasting mountains.   Hear its heavy groans—
the groans of an expiring world, as breaks its heart
within its bosom.   The azure curtain that's behind
the sun, encompassing the earth as does a mantle, is
shrivelled up.   The fierceness of the flames crumples
it as bark of tree is shrivelled up on a fiery burning
hearth.   The air is choked with densest clouds
ascending dark.   Flames burst forth in curling
volumes circling round on every side, around the globe,
the thunders roll.   Crash after crash is heard.   The
flames consume the glory of the skies, as fire devours
the heath on mountain's side.   And to increase the
fury of the storm, from heaven's four quarters come
the rushing winds, fanned by the breath of angels
great in might, to hasten on the consummation of all
things.   Quickly the flames devour.   The six days'
works that God had made, are by their fierceness all
dissolved.   But Oh ! how rich thy stores, Thou Mighty
King !   The loss of a thousand worlds will not be
missed by Thee.   All is now in grasp of death.
Creation all is turned upside down.

Now the Judge decides each case.   The doom of
all mankind by Him is fixed.   From highest heavens
He descends, seated upon His throne, clothed with
majesty and glory never seen.   His glory all Divine,
Him round about as with a garment clothes.   He

holds a thousand thunders in His hand, in wrath
to punish all His daring foes. See how these
thunders quiver, how they pant to be let loose to execute His will, as hounds do long to be let loose from
leash, to seize upon their prey. Innumerable angels
throng His court. They fix their thoughts upon the
orders of their King. They run at His command to
execute the same.

Thou Judas now appear. Let all appear who
did with thee conspire in thy horrific deed. Appear,
all ye who did deny the faith of Christ the Lord, and
sold Him for a thing of nought. Ye senseless ones
who made your choice of gold—who it preferred to
God, and to the glories and the joys of Paradise
Divine. Your foolish barter now behold. See the
destruction on yourselves ye bring. Ye haughty
ones, dupes of mistaken shame—abashed that ye
should hear the voice of praise and thanksgiving to
God within your homes. Behold the glory of the
King, and wonder not from His domains to see yourselves eternally debarred. Herod come thou. Behold the king that thou didst scorn, and in mockery
of His Royalty in purple garments clothed. Behold
Him now earth's Judge. Behold His Royal robes,
those scarlet flames in which He is arrayed. He
comes their righteous portion to the good to give—the
wicked to consume in wrath. And Pilate raise thou
thine eye aloft. See the mutation great. Wilt thou
believe that this is He whom at thy partial bar, thou
didst condemn! nor would'st set free, though conscience
warned thee of His innocence. Believest thou that
head to be the blessèd head on which in mockery was

pressed the prickly thorn. Is this the face that was
defiled with loathsome spittle of the Jews? Oh!
tragedy unparalleled. The sun did hide His face.
Refuse he did to be a witness to the horrid deed.
Oh! how was it that all creation did not die, when
thus its Lord was crucified upon the tree!

His mighty angels He sends forth. They quickly
gather to His throne the habitants of earth. Each
one they bring. From east, from west, from north,
from south, they come. Quickly they come.
Almighty power them gathers to the great tribunal of
their God. All that in flesh did e'er dwell, from east,
from west, they quickly come, as swarms of bees that
cluster round a branch, together come they, summoned
forth by God's command.

A glorious angel shall uplift on high the banner of
our Saviour King—the banner of Christ whose badge
is blood. He summons them who 'neath its shade did
trust, who in His sufferings great their trust did put.
Says He, my saints let gathered be to me. Let all those
come who of my covenant of grace laid hold—all those
who in faith—sincerity—submission true, attached
themselves to me. Then the Judge to the great work
proceeds—His enemies righteously to judge. The
books He then unfolds, in which the deeds of men
recorded are. The secrets of men's hearts He also
does reveal. He shews to each the horrid thoughts
that lay within his breast. He these lays open, that
every one may see what lay within the secret chamber
of his heart. When thus they see themselves.
When thus they see themselves revealed. When thus
they see themselves exposed. When thus they see
the purity of justice all Divine; dissolved in shame

is every face, burning with shame as with the torment of consuming fire.

Then the trumpet sounds again commanding silence to observe. Not one may speak or move; that all may hear the judgment now pronounced on great and small. " Ye covetous who the right forsook, who hope in wealth reposed—your hearts who fast locked up. Ye who your ears did close 'gainst piteous cries of poor afflicted ones. The naked did not clothe, the hungry did not feed, though I your garners did replenish, and did increase your flocks each year. Devoid of mercy, truth, and love, unfit are ye to share my heritage. From off your souls my image ye have torn. For ever for your woes yourselves accuse—for your destruction everlasting. Oh! ye profane ones; ye who imprecated, and impiously prayed, that Satan would your souls possess. Now it is time to grant your wish. Nor can you ever say your doom's unjust. Ye who your tongues did set on edge—as knives that sharpened are, evil to speak, to slander, to backbite, to lie, and God blaspheme. Oh! ye destructive serpents, horrible, and grim ye look. How can I bear your reptile hissing sounds, or hope to hear sweet notes of praise from forkèd tongues, with . deadliest poison all bedewed.

" Ye who contemned my holy ordinance—nor loved the house of prayer—to whom when listening to my law, an hour in my abode was wearisome and long as if a year. How can ye relish an everlasting sabbath in my service? How can your souls delight in that to which your very nature hatred bears?

Ye malevolent and envious ones to whom prosperity of others was a torment—who gnawed your tongues, at sight of one that prospered more than you —how can you inherit happiness in glory—full bliss enjoy, where ye myriads see, exalted high above your heads, in these my realms. Would not malice,— would not envy, kindle in your souls the flame of hell, even in the precincts of my heavenly paradise, when such a sight ye see.

" Ye who in deeds unchaste indulged—specially ye the marriage bed who did defile. Ye my holy law who did despise, abandoning yourselves to carnal fleshly lusts. As in the heat and passion of corrupt desire ye did delight to revel, for you is now by me prepared a fiery bed whereon to lie, in linen sheets of reddest flame. Though I should bring you to my glory; 'twere as the bringing in of swine, to the royal palace of a King. Your hearts impure would even there tormented be, gnawed by your starving lusts, for lack of their congenial food.

" Ye who meet are for my realm, on my right take your stand. And ye who are as fruitless trees 'mong fruitful ones on my left let your position be. Thus, as a shepherd separates his flocks; separates the fleecy sheep, from fleeceless goats; so He does separate the righteous ones—His own, from those that are of Satan's flock. Then shall He say to them who on His right do stand, come ye, prepared and saved of grace. Come and inherit ye the kingdom that for you I have prepared, where joy in fulness is, pleasures for evermore. By my obedience perfect, and my sufferings great, I burst the gate that shut you out. For in my side an entrance wide, the spear

L

has oped, an entrance new for you thereby to enter in. Approach with joy the Tree of life in Paradise Divine; and test its virtues marvellous, your every sore and wound to heal. The sword unsheathed —the fiery sword that it did guard on every side, therefrom our parents Adam and Eve excluding, for that very sword, of my heart a sheathe I've made, and quenched its fiery flame by mine own blood. Beneath its verdant branches whose bright bloom shall ne'er decay, do ye yourselves repose, and as thrushes in the woodland bower, then sing the heavenly praises of your Saviour King. Its beauty let your eye delight. The heat can ne'er you hurt, beneath its shade. From its fragrant healing leaves, salvation everlasting have, and from its wondrous fruit imbibe a happy blessed immortality. Each tree within the Paradise of God is unforbidden now to you, eat fearlessly from every branch, the lurking serpent never more can sting. Now to the full your heart's desire in God indulge. He of truth the fountain is— of mercy also and of love, remaining full through ages yet to come. The great and wondrous scheme by which you're saved—its length and breadth do ye explore. Yea, with all my works, in my dominion vast, do ye yourselves acquaint, and new delights drink in, knowing more and more. Your joy let ever grow—your beauty, understanding, and your love, let them increase throughout the endless ages of eternity. And let there never cross your path, what will give pain or vex your soul. Eye hath not seen, nor ear hath heard, the joys I've treasured up for you. Go, and let your experience of the same, continually attest the truth of these felicities that are your heritage."

But the party on his left, in vengeance dire He thus addresses. "Ye who no love to God did cherish, depart to the devil. From me depart. My curse, let it for ever cling to you, that your lot may ever be one of pain and torment. Go into the awful fire, that there consumed for ever you may be. And forthwith as the earth did cleave asunder, to swallow Korah and his wicked crew ; so shall the pit of hell's abyss its mouth wide open, panting to receive its prey. And as the monstrous whale did swallow Jonas up, when cast he was into the sea, ev'n so the second death's dark, wide open mouth, shall swallow them and crush them by its iron jaws. In this den so horrible, shall be associated in bands, the various workers of iniquity—swearers profane—the murderers—and they who witness false did bear—drunkards, and robbers, and adulterers. Like bundles of the prickly thorn, that dry and shrivelled are, fast bound by cords, so is each class of sinners bound by chains apart ; and those in wicked fellowship that once were joined, are now as naked goads piercing each other's sides. As lions fierce by chains restrained, do ply their tusks to break the tie, so they ever gnaw their chains, but never can their teeth the brazen fetters break. For evermore in the dark embrace of death, with grief their wretched hearts continually are wrung. On an ocean of burning sulphur, bound they are. The vapours green their nostrils ever choke. Like limpets fastened to the rock they fastened are on the cliffs of this boiling main, and the great wind of God's wrath boils it up, into boisterous billows o'er

their heads. Soon as in sleep their eyes they close,
so soon they startled are, from their repose. The
heat of wrath Divine, and dark despair, of them
possession take anew—the worm that dies not, as the
heat of burning coals, shall multiply and multiply
anew their everlasting pains. When thus of the pit
they full possession get, and come to know and realise
what tribute they must surely pay, in some such
doleful words as these, we may describe their sad
bemoaning of themselves.

" From the state of nothing, wherein I had my rest,
why did God exalt my head ? My thousand curses
on the day my mother me conceived. Why did I
understanding ever get ? Why did I sense or reason
ever get, my steps to guide ? Why didst thou not a
fly me make, or a humble worm, that crawls in the
lowly dust ? For ages—through ages all, must I exist
in this my doleful state ? Shall not my end for ever
come—or any change my misery relieve ? Oh ! is it
so that I am now in the eternity that endless is—
swimming on its shoreless ocean ! Could I number all
the stars, could I count each blade of grass, and every
leaf that in the forest ever grew, could I number
every drop that fills the ocean great, and count each
grain of sand that circles it around ; and were I to
pass a thousand years for each of these, no more of
vast eternity is gone than if it yesterday began !

" But Oh ! is Heavenly mercy at an end ! From
age to age will God torment ! Will He never slacken
these my chains—these manacles, will He not lose
for ever off my hands ! Will the mouth that God
ordained to sing throughout all ages, and proclaim

His praise unweariedly, be like a pair of bellows, fanning up green flames in hell beneath! But though my woe exceed my strength, in truth I must confess my sentence to be just. How long shall I be here, in misery and pain, before Thy justice strict is satisfied? Or wilt Thou ever be avenged upon me? Has nature's law been laid aside. Alas! Alas! is this the second death, which Thou on Adam didst denounce at first. To satisfy Thy vengeance, shalt Thou spin, and smaller spin, throughout eternity this slender thread of life in me? Will it not suffice, that I a thousand years should burn for every sin that I was guilty of? Though to the very utmost, wrath pursue me, this cannot exalt Thy praise, Oh! God. Beneath Thy majesty, it is, to deign, Thy wrath to vent on me so poor an object. Oh God, wilt Thou not annihilate me, and by Thy mighty power put my soul at once out of being? Cast me from Thee into a state of nonentity, where neither work, nor thought, nor suffering is. But Oh! this is my own desert, nor am I unjustly dealt with. For, Christ so freely offered I refused. His precious blood I did despise. My conscience ever me condemns, the witness true that always me accused. Nor will it permit me, suffering though I am, ever ascribe to God, either cruelty or injustice, though He on me this death inflicts. His holy law I utterly despised. 'Gainst its warnings, I trod destruction's ways. I smothered the living monitor that He placed within my breast; and to my welfare clearly shown, I shut my eyes. Who can measure the vengeance due to me for sins so dreadful, and so bold; sins which at defiance set

the blood of Jesus Christ, and left to me no efficacy
in His precious death ! But are not all thine attri-
butes eternal, infinite, and can my guilt cause love
and mercy to have end in God ? Canst Thou cast
me far away, where Thine ear won't hear my moan ?
Or is there darkness ev'n in hell, that can my state
conceal from Thee. Filled with happiness ineffable as
Thou art, wilt Thou not bend Thine ear to hear my
voice—the cry of a poor creature which Thy hand has
formed, crying aloud, Oh ! Father pity have on me,
and intermit this heat that boils the marrow of my
bones ! Oh ! my God hear my piteous pleadings—the
mournful sighs that usher from my breast. This one
request I do of Thee implore. When for each sin I
ever did commit, ten thousand years I here shall weep,
tormented in this fiery flame ; when devils have
tired of torturing me, *O God do grant that then I die.*
But this my agonizing prayer shall not be heard ; nor
rest nor peace can I obtain, but life immortal still increasing, constantly imparted to strengthen me, now
and increasing pain to bear."

But stop my song, retrace thy steps, ascend from
the abyss of woe unutterable. See how thou canst
direct the living to escape this awful fate, that they
may not go down.

Reader is all this true ? Do you believe what's
written in my song ? If indeed it be as I have said,
come, Oh ! come, and bend the knee in penitential
prayer. Make no delay. To Jesus instantly betake
thyself. Abhor, forsake the ways of sin. By faith
sincere embrace, and do thyself submit to Him,—to
all the commandments of His holy law. In all His

offices Him receive; omitting none.   Receive Him as
thy Prophet, Priest, and King,—for guidance, for
salvation, and for strength,   Let His example regu-
late thy ways; and in accord therewith thy conduct
frame.   And all the means ordained by Him that
sinners should be saved, these diligently use.   Not
one despise.   In His righteousness alone repose thy
trust.   Never depend on merit of thine own.   And
if it be thy true desire, that grace should efficacious
prove, harbour no darling sin within thy breast.
Then though thy guilt be great, to the glory of thy
Lord, thou shalt indeed be saved.   And to fill thy
soul with bliss· ineffable, thou shalt for ever and for
ever sing the praises of thy Saviour King.

THE DREAM.

CONTENTS :—Sleep—The vision—The address—Man's disappointments—
The reason of this—Vanity of earthly pleasures—This true of every
class—The reason of this—Lust insatiable—Christianity only capable
of yielding true happiness.

While I lay fast asleep, dreaming as others do, vain
and empty dreams,—seeking happiness from fleeting things; and which as soon as I supposed I had,
quickly vanished from my grasp.   Methinks that one
came nigh to me thus whispering in mine ear.   "Oh!
foolish man, what dost thou mean?   Canst thou catch
the wind?   Canst thou hold it in thine hand?   Think-
est thou the world can satisfy thy heart?   'Tis vain
for thee to seek for peace in anything or plan, beneath
the sun.   Thy body rests not on this side the grave;

nor is there rest for your immortal soul, but only in
the Lord.   Once Adam ate of the forbidden fruit, sin
as a canker entered everything—made everything a
labour sore, the world a heartbreak to us all.   He
forfeited the happiness of his soul, the pleasures that
in Paradise he enjoyed.   Since then mankind unhappy are and poor—like lambs that from their
mothers and the fold, astray have gone.   Bleating
hard because of what they miss, each object they
pursue, and vainly try to find in it the rest, that they
so sorely miss.   But in it no rest they find.   To them
the world is cold and pityless as unsympathising stepmother to children not her own.   Thus they are tossed
about, restless, reposeless, weary with their efforts
vain to catch a fleeting shadow, trying in vain to
suck the milk of happiness from earthly objects, dry
as is the barren breast within the infant's lips.

" From some anxiety or want you're never free.
Hope decoys you on, in vain expecting sure relief,
which always seems within your grasp.   It seems not
further off from you than an arm's length.   But still
you never do succeed in getting it.   Soon as you
think you have it, it eludes you.   Nor does your sore
experience you suffice to teach, not to confide in expec-
tations vain which have a thousand times deceived, and
are to-day as far away as yesterday.   Have you never
found the object that you most desired, most bitter prove
in the fruition of it ?   Expectation gives more joy
than does a Royal crown in actual possession !—which
fades, as fades the blooming rose when it is pulled.
Its beauty and its fragrance soon begin to die, just as
you take it in your hand.   Not one 'mong all

the sons of men, is from trouble free.   The sighs of
Majesty as many are as those of men of lowest grade.
From each burning faggot its curling smoke ascends.
And side by side with fair prosperity sits dark adver-
sity.   The rose grows on the prickly thorn, and side
by side you find the honey and the sting.

"When the affluent you see flourishing in their
state.   Think not that happiness is their's beyond
what others have not, in possession of such wealth.
The purest fountain welling up its chrystal streams,
has sediment beneath.   If agitate the well you do, as
hastily its waters you suck up.   Soon shall the dregs
arise, and fill thy mouth with gravel and with sand.
Though one you see in high estate, and envy his repose,
he's but a nest in lofty tree, which threatened is by
every passing tempest ; and tossed by every wind that
blows.   The man on whom the world its brightest
smiles doth lavish, has a defficiency—a crook,
which neither wisdom nor device of his can cure.
'Tis as a staff that crooked is, part bending against
part, whose shape you can't undo.   As surely as you
straighten the one end, forthwith the other you will
bend.   The Jews the manna gathered on the plain—
that blessed food that down from heaven was sent.
Some gathered more, some gathered less.   The man
that gathered much had nothing o'er ; and he that
gathered little had no lack.   So all the prosperity and
enjoyment man can have on earth.   Over against all—
riches, courtly dignities, and stations high, there's
waste and care and grief.   Though in your shell
accumulate you may great wealth, you'll find that by
its side the lead accumulates, and should you put a

kingdom in the other scale, e'en that would fail the balance to restore.   Each one his fitting portion has received.   And though you think 'twere better you had more ; you'll find that the abundance you desire cannot diminish in the very least the crushing pressure of your grief.   Inconstancy of mind and heart begets your pain.   You now refuse what yesterday so eagerly you sought.   The world can't possibly satisfy your contradictory desires—your continuous cross purposes.   If the flesh is to be gratified and its desires all satiated, no other heaven will it seek, than wallow in base lusts for evermore.   And yet while thus you doat on earthly pleasures, your vanity and pride prompt you to rise as high as the throne of God. But if you wish for lasting happiness, dedicate thyself and ways to God in faith, sincerity and love ; and then to thee He'll truly give, all thine heart's desire. Along with this He'll give all that of happiness the world can bestow—food, raiment, health, peace, lovingkindness—salvation great for evermore."   Then I awoke.   My dream was gone.   I ceased to grasp at shadows vain, and I became contented with my lot.

THE HERO.

CONTENTS :—Alexander the Great—Cæsar—The hero is he who overcomes fear—Meets ills courageously—By the blood of Christ quiets an accusing conscience—His sobriety—His virtue—Dead to the world— Dead to lust—Inward peace—Soliloquy—Conclusion.

ALEXANDER THE GREAT was no hero—nor Cæsar, though Rome he subdued.   O'er others, though triumphs they won, the slaves of their lusts they remained. To slaughter multitudes is no true heroism, nor is it glory to be oft on battle field. Nor is it greatness to be fierce and proud.

But he the hero is, who overcomes the fears of life, and terrors of grim death; and who with dauntless courage ever meets his destiny whatever him befals. From guilty fears he will not flee away. When conscience wakes and him assails, her accusations all he hears to end; and with the pleadings of atoning blood he answers all. He is the hero, who his will subjects to reason true; and who his thoughts to right and just demands subjects. His brutal lusts he tramples under foot, and in submission to God's law them keeps—as in subjection to the head the members of the body are. Nor does He condescend, that those should reign whose part it is to yield and to obey. At night when lies he down to sleep, his virtues watch do keep around, as faithful soldiers watch their king, from enemies him to guard. At morn from slumber when he wakes, his thoughts together gathers he; and as a skilful general at their head, he marshals them, that he may battle do, and fight against his carnal lusts—'gainst poverty and every worldly woe—'gainst stratagems, and deadly snares by Satan laid to ruin men. His soul is fixed as on a rock. Nor fear, nor terror him disturbs. His eye is ever vigilant, and quick to see the hook, through bait which it so skilfully conceals. In vain the world displays its glory—wealth, its honours all in one. Riches and honour in his heart he has, which he for crowned royalty will not exchange.

Though the harlot spread her net, with her beauty's snares him to allure. Her eye nor dazzles him, nor can her flaming lust his resolution shake. Though sorely prest at times he is, yet over him his foe does not prevail. When weak and bruised in heart then is he strong, and on his knees he gets the victory. His helmet is the truth in purity, and faith in Jesus is his shield. The word of God is as his sharp two-edged sword, and all his hope does rest in Him alone. Within his soul he has an inward peace, for by the blood of Christ his conscience cleansed is. Thus, he possesses riches that the world has not the power to give; that will last, when earth and all its glory pass away.

He will not bend his ear to flattery. Nor can vile slander take away his inward peace. Neither do heavy tidings him dismay. Neither can slander wound his heart.

Awake my soul, thine armour put thou on. This mighty hero emulate. Thy lusts subdue, and in subjection keep. A kingdom conquer thou within thyself. Let thy affections soar above the clouds, 'tis a poor heritage that is beneath the sun. View earth but as a little verdant knoll; and men like ants encompassing it round. To and fro, restless they go, to gather stores to fill their chest. They trample on each other, as in their haste they move, and fiercely struggle for a broken reed. The world when thus thou hast surveyed, raise up thy thoughts from earth beneath, that wealth thou mayest possess—both peace and joy within thyself, that nevermore shall end.

THE SKULL.

As I sat by a grave surveying the same, behold an unsightly skull. The relic I raised, and with feelings so sad, I turned it round. No beauty it had nor hue, No knowledge nor thought, of any that passed its way. Toothless its mouth, silent its tongue, nor had it a throat as was wont sweetly to sing. No flush on its cheek. No locks adorn its brow; nor is there an ear to hear my song. Of smell no sense remains. Former things are passed away. Lidless the eye. No brightness is there. No vision to guide, as was wont. Empty the eyeless sockets. By worms these eyes are eaten away. Into dust the brain is changed ! No scheme or plan to relieve its wants has it now. No thought is there of retracing its steps to right its wrongs. Thy face cannot tell who thou wert— whether King or Duke. Alexander the Great is alike with the hungry slave, who on loathsome dunghill, died without food.

Grave-digger come nigh ! whisper now in mine ear whose skull I in my hand do hold; that I may him ask what his way in the past, though echo he'll never my song.

Wert thou a comely maid with a beautiful face and form—a bright glowing eye—thy beauty a net that captured each youth that thee saw. Thy charms are

all gone that gained thee homage of love.   They're to
loathsomeness turned.   Accursed be the grave that
despoiled thee of beauty and grace, that once thee
adorned.

Wert thou a judge both upright and just, clear
sighted and true, who justice dispensed to friend and
foe ?   Impartial, unswayed, would'st judge to the death
whatever deserved the same ?   Or didst thou the right
forego for " sordid gains "—when bribed by such as by
wealth could enrich, whilst the poor who sought thy
protection were trampled upon, because thy favours
they had not the means to buy ?   If thou didst not
faithful prove. .   If thou didst partial judgment give
perverting the right.   As surely as so you did :
condemned you were, when at God's bar on high,
appear you did.

Or a Physician hast thou been ; skilled to cure, a
healer of wounds—and diseases all, that man can as-
sail ; boasting thy cures infallible—professing to rescue
from death itself, its prey ?   Alas ! Alas ! that thy
skill thee forsaken has, when sore assailed, at that
suffering hour.   Nor plaster nor purge could avail to
heal, or redeem thee one hour from the grave.

A commander hast thou been, renowned for thy
skill in arms and war—leading forth thy men, thy foes
to subdue, by thousands them slaying, strewing thy
path with heaps of dying and dead ?   Thy sword its
power, how has it lost ?—or thy hand its wonted
strength, when met thee the host of the grave !   When
despite of power and skill, yield thee thou must to an
army of crawling worms.   These worms thee besiege, and
on thee feast each day.   Thy skull where once ambitious

thoughts dwelt, is now a garrison made for the lowly beetle there to abide.   Thy sapping and mining skill is matched by the tiny worms.   Some bore thy teeth. Some tear thine ears.   Some issue in swarms from thine eyes, to ravage thy cheeks, and carry away the spoil.

Or a bibber of wine wert thou, who oft did the tavern frequent to fill thyself with drink, as you merrily quaffed the deadly bowl ?   Thy heaven it was, nor didst thou e'er covet of bliss or of God than just, that thy brain should swim in its fumes.   The music that's sweetest to thee are oaths—horrid oaths—thy Maker's name to blaspheme, and in brutal display of strength, trying whose is the hardest fist.   Senseless art thou and shameless as horse or cow—debased by lust as there in your vomit you are, in midst of your cups.

Or is it the skull of a man, who sober and faithful was—at whose table temperance reigned—whose virtues with graces attendant ever bore rule—Who appetite kept in control at the festal board, when there he sat with friends?

Or a glutton wert thou, aye greedy of meat as dogs of flesh—indulging thy lust unsatiable, and making thy belly thy god ?   That belly of thine to which as a god thou didst bow, of earth and of sand is full.   Thy jaws fast locked are now, and thy tongue without taste is fast bound in the brazen fetters of death.

Or is it the skull of a Lord that has chanced to come to hand—Once the owner of land ?   Who with his wealth was kind to the poor—the naked he clothed that needed his help.   Or sordid wert thou—with severity sore fleecing thy tenants—grinding them down with rents—seizing their flocks, when their poverty earnest-

ly pled for respite to pay ?   They dare not before thee
stand though shorn of their locks by age, without
bonnet in hand to honour thy haughty head though
the frozen wintry blast their ears should bite.   Now
thy slave may approach, nor do homage nor fear thee,
now despoiled as thou art of thy wealth, thine honour,
thy court.   High praise be to death, that has laid its
arrest on thee, and endures not thy pride and power
beneath the sod.

Or a minister of Christ wert thou who earnestly
pled with his flock in God's name,—who entreated
the sinner to turn, who the broadway to death and to
hell did pursue ?   Or cold and heartless wert thou in
thy calling—not tending the flock of God, but acting
the stepmother cold ?   If the fleece thou didst get, the
fox the flock may guide.   Then sure I'm of this, that
thy deeds their reward did receive—when the Chief
Shepherd you met—when summoned by death, in His
presence to stand—to render account of thy talents
received.

Or is it a skull once full of deadly schemes, framing
thy plans and boldly putting forth the same, without
fear or awe of God Most High ?   Didst thou harbour
the lying tongue unrestrained within thy mouth ?   Did
it wound with its venomous sting ? as a serpent
that bites, such as within its reach that are.   It is now
at rest silent beneath the curb of death, never more
its slanders to spread as a plague through the land.
The loathsome worms have consumed it quite, to rot
in its place in their turn.   If so you lived till death
thy head did lay low, nor didst repent in time, truth
to embrace.   In this grave for a season abide.   'Tis

all the heaven you'll have, till summoned to meet thy God. Then like a black crawling frog from the pit, you'll ascend to appear in presence of Christ the Judge, when He comes again, thine evil deeds to requite. When thou shalt be tried before His throne, and thy sentence pronounced, then justice condemns thee to die—to be banished for ever from the presence of God. Thy lot is eternal flames of fire—fire for the devil prepared. God's curse shall for ever pursue, as a foe pursues a foe to slay. Then God will harden thy bones as iron—thy veins as brazen thongs. Thy flesh shall become as an anvil hard which hammers have threshed—which heat however intense can never dissolve.

But wert thou a head in which wisdom and sense dwelt—that knew thy God, and did what was right and pleasing to Him. Albeit this day tho' naked thou art, bereft of knowledge and light to guide—without tongue to speak—or eyes to see—or nose to smell. Take courage ev'n now in the grave though thou'rt low. . Thou shalt rise with joy at the noise of the sounding trump. Thy corruption and filth behind thou shalt leave to the loathsome worms of the pit. Then as the sun in the morning dawn that shines on the wings of the mountains—thy beauty shall be. Such beauty, thy God shall for thee prepare. He'll put sight in those eyes. They will shine as bright stars in thy head. Thy tongue He'll unloose, and thy throat He'll attune to sing God's praise in His court. He'll open thine ear to hear how the heavenly hosts His glorious name do praise. When Christ comes again, in His glory to shine, and gather His righteous ones to His mansions on high. Then thou shalt leap thy Lord to meet as swift as the eagle does fly. Aloft thou shalt rise, thy welcome then comes. Christ shall thee welcome to friendship eternal enjoy. You two shall part no more. His communion of love shall ever be thine, His Paradise high. Whoever thou art, that hearest my song, delay make none—repent. Repent while reason remains—while health still endures. Repent before death on thee seize. And if in thy sins it thee finds, never more shalt thou enter the gate of salvation and grace.

WINTER.

CONTENTS :—Effects of winter described—The misery of such as failed to foresee and provide against it—Exhortation to the careless—Old age described—Address to the young—Uncertainty of life—The folly and misery of dying without Christ—Conclusion.

BRIGHT summer is gone, and winter 's approaching —that inveterate foe of all growth is come—our country to spoil,—to strip it of beauty—to trample it all 'neath his feet. Without mercy or favour he comes to blight and plunder our land. His wings he has spread o'er our heads. The sun he has hidden behind him. From the nest he has taken the brood. Without mercy he lashes. White feathery snow he showers from the clouds. Hail driven by winds from the north fast flies around us, like discharges of powder and shot. The blast of his mouth when he blows, leaves no life in a flower. His lips are as scissors. Of the bloom of their roses, each garden he strips. Of their beautiful green each forest he strips.

'Neath blue flags of ice each torrent he stems. A
frozen tempest issues from his throat; it blows into
a hurricane. The ocean it ferments. ` Its mighty
billows roll. On heights of mountains he the sleet
congeals. He burnished hath the stars, that with
their lustre dazzled have our eyes.

` Each man, each beast, that have forgot in their
due season to provide, lashed by the tempest are. They
naked are and houseless, by tempest they're pursued.
The busy ones who gathered in their stores, are
careful them to keep, and scant are of compassion ;
lest they scarce should prove. To the slothful lend
they won't, tho' perish in the snow from want should
be.

The ant, the bee, have gathered in their stores.
With wisdom wonderful the storm foresaw. They
lack not. On food and honey they are fed, and in
their shelter they're protected, nor do they feel the
breezing blast.

But the airy flies, that danced their summer in the
shining sun, who no thought had 'gainst winter to
provide. Behold them now. See how from want
they perish everywhere.

Hark thee, old man ! What my parable means
do thou note. Death is approaching apace. That
is the winter of my song. If thee it finds a sluggard
—unprepared to meet him ; thy last regrets will not
avail, nor save thee from the coming tempest. 'Tis
time to turn to God ; for hoary are thy locks become.
Behold the breaches in thy teeth. See how with age
thy face is dry and puckered up. Thy brow is pale and
bare. Thine eyes are bleared. The heavy load of

life, for years by thee borne, thy back has bent.   Thou art bending down, to thy native bed of earth.   The crimson streams that erst so merrily careered through all thy limbs, are ebbing fast.   Once flowing lively, briskly through each pulse.   Now their flow is almost gone.   Thy spirits cease to flow.   Sluggish the action of thy blood both stiff and cold, no more impelling thee as once it did.   The bellows of thy life is useless now and worn.   In thy breast it is contracted. And painful is the blowing of it.   Thy body is a stringed instrument which can't be tuned.   Its music is gone.   Nothing is left but discord.   Loose are its strings ; a sign that soon committed it shall be, to the dark and lonesome grave.   The gay morning of youth is departed.   Meridian strength is away.   Thy sun is declining.   The shadows of evening are lowering, and night is approaching.   If in the past you were heedless, idling thy day of grace ; quickly arouse thee, or salvation is gone for ever.   As we spend our life, with most so it ends.   Habits grow stronger.   Their roots spread further and deeper. They untwine them around us in folds that cannot be broken.   As is said in the proverb, 'tis indeed a true saying.   " The tree that twisted grows is rarely straightened. "

Oh ! ardent young man, now hear my song.   From folly Oh ! cease, and thy youth give to God.   Old age comes apace.   Disease is pursuing thee fast.   If it thee surprise in folly's dark path ; converted to sorrow thy joys shall then be.   Unknown are the wounds that old age will inflict.   Thine eyes it misty shall make.   It will plough thy face with wrinkles deep.

Thy glossy locks with hoar frost it shall sprinkle;
and on thy countenance imprint the hue of death.
Nor sun nor thaw can dissolve this frost.   But more
than this.   Thy powers of mind decay.   Reason fails.
Thine understanding is impaired.   Its eyes grow dim.
Thy memory wanes.   Thy vigour and powers of mind
are gone.   Capacity for business is gone.   Thy senses
lose their force and charms.   In thy body and thy
mind infantile thou'rt become.   While thus you
feeble grow, thy heart grows hard—ever less disposed
to change—to hear instruction's warning voice; or
yield to her entreaties.   As the hard and frozen
earth in winter, so is the hardened heart.   Thousands
its surface tread, but not the vestige of a footstep
remains behind.   Consider the several seasons of the
year, and from the works of nature wisdom learn.
The husbandman must till and sow in spring, or
harvest will him yield no crop.   In summer we store
up our fuel to protect us from cold in winter.   If this
you neglect then comfort you'll want.   In the spring
of thy youth, if good seed you neglect to sow in your
heart.   The enemy surely will come; and in it his
tares he will sow.   'Tis as sure as the advent of
death, that so he will do, and that sinful seed will
wickedness produce—the carnal herbs that surely will
grow.   For as you sow so shalt thou reap.   From
virtue, virtue grows, and vice from vice.   If unruly
in thy youth.   If unbridled are thy passions.
Wilder and wilder they shall grow.   Nor can they
by age be subdued.   If when but 'tis a plant you
cannot twist a tree; much less can you uproot it,
when 'tis grown.   As its boughs extend so do its roots,
and fasten firmer, deeper in ground.

Uncertain is our life.   Uncertain is it when or how we life may leave.   Now to thy God be reconciled.   Give diligence to have it so.   Delay not for an hour.   Delay is fatal.   Its thousands it has slain.   To put thy salvation off till a dying hour and then expect it, as hopeless is, as to expect returns from sowings done 'mid wintry frosts and snows.   The sun each day his course does run.   Each night he sets.   Each night and day curtails the span of life.   As swiftly as the shuttle runs through the web ; the web of life as quickly woven is, and soon shall thy shroud be finished, and dressed in it thou shalt the food of worms become.   And if death will o'ertake thee unexpected, thou wilt open thine eyes to find thyself irretrievably lost.   For penitence no place is found.   As dagger struck into thy heart, so conscience will torment thy spirit.   To endure it is, as if you were naked laid on a bed of thorns.   Behold the summer fly.   By laws of nature 'tis condemned.   Its opportunity it did neglect, and now by wintry tempests 'tis condemned to penalty of death.   Behold and learn from wisdom of the ant, which timely preparation made.   Go to the ant thou sluggard.   Go and likewise do, and let thy soul be saved.

THE PRAYER.

CONTENTS :—Address to the Deity—Self-abasement—The sinner's desert— The atoning refuge—Resignation sought—Trust in Christ—Spiritual-mindedness—Unreserved confidence in God through Christ.

OH ! Thou most glorious God ! Thou high exalted one.

Thou King of kings. How solemn 'tis for lips un-
clean Thy Great and Holy name to mention. The
Highest Angels in thy Heavenly Host, compared with
Thee, are weak in strength, and blind their sight!
How little know they of Thy Mighty works! How
far surpassing all their praise of Thee, is Thy glory
infinite! compared with purity Divine, the brightest
stars are dim. Nor spotless are the Highest, Holiest
Angels when stand they do before Thy glorious throne.

Oh! wilt Thou condescend? Wilt Thou lend an ear
to hear a worm on earth, a dweller at Thy footstool,
one who only sees a little shadow of Thy face. Oh!
everlasting God, let not thine anger kindled be when
now I pour my prayer out—when sin with shame
to Thee I do confess—the abominable transgression
of which I have been guilty. My guilt is as the
mountains high. On me it has inflicted many wounds.
The burden of my sins has crushed my soul, and from
mine eye has wrung the bitter tear.

Eternal God, canst Thou me save, and not ignore
Thy justice great? And if to me, Thou mercy shalt extend, can this be done, without reflection on thy
character and God-head true? Nay, does not justice
strict demand unless denied, that I for evermore
should perish. My dreadful guilt has scarcely left
Thee room that mercy or grace on me Thou should'st
bestow. All the curses of the law that written are,
all dreadful threatenings denounced against the guilty,
Lord I deserve them at Thy hand. My doom is just,
though heaped these curses were, for ever on my head.
Though Heavens frown in wrath, tho' prostrate low I
should be laid, by thunder of Thy power. Though

down to hell Thou should'st me cast, Thy justice ev'n in doing it I am compelled to own.

But 'neath the shelter of Emmanuel's blood I'm safe. There the fiery flame, the mighty flame by which the floods asunder riven are, cannot me reach,— cannot affect me, covered as I am by the obedience of Christ. In His atoning blood, the blood that satisfied inexorable justice, the blood that fell to earth from Calvary's cross—in it I put my trust, Oh! King, my King—that for its sake, my soul thou wilt absolve from guilt. In this atoning Saviour let me ingrafted be. Then my withered tree shall flourish—with bud and blossom shall break forth. Then Holy virtues like the fruit the bow that bends, shall me adorn.

Whatever be my lot beneath the sun, daily my God make me contented with Thy will. If poor or rich, if sick or whole, thy will be ever done by me. All that God gives—of grace He gives—of favour free to guilty undeserving man. When also He with- holds, it is in love. His every cross, He lays on His —His every deprivation He inflicts a blessing is—a blessing in a mask. Thanks to Thee, O gracious God, a glorious Saviour who to me did'st send, in whose atoning death the ransom of my liberty I find; and in whose blood I see the price of my redemption and the infinite preciousness of the soul. In the healing fountain from His side that flowed do Thou, Oh! God of peace, me cleanse. In this is life from death. In this is liberty from bondage of corruption that me enthralls. In His atoning death my faith confirm. Kindle flame of love Divine within my heart. And strengthen thou me with might in the inner man obedience true to render, and submission to all the precepts of His law.   All this I truly owe to Him. He it was that 'neath the dreadful load of all my sins His back did bend to lay it on.   All which He did to raise my bowed broken spirit up to God.   The many gifts that I enjoy—the many precious benefits I have cost Him—each one of them—many a piercing pang, and many a heavy sigh.

Raise my earthly thoughts.   To heaven them elevate.   Fix them on heavenly things.   Confer on me the earnest of Thy love—that love which banishes my fear—that love that with sweet assurance fills my soul, and gives me comfort, when thinking of the gloomy hour of death.   Then let ocean's turgid billows roll. Let heaven's thunder peal along the sky.   Let earth with earthquakes quake and tremble.   Come famine, or come plague that carries death whithersoever it goes. If Thou shalt be my God all these in loving friendship shall remain.   No power the fire has to consume— nor can the ocean swallow up—nor can the plague destroy without permission from Thy throne. While power almighty with my God remains, from every evil I'm secure.   Nor will I fear that ever want I'll have— or that the fulness of Thy stores shall fail.   All my desires do centre in my God.   My will is in subjection to His word.   My fears are subject to Him—all meet in Him.   For heaven, and earth, and hell beneath, are under His control who is my King.

THE SKULL.

As I sat by a grave,
Surveying the same,
A Skull I perceived on the ground ;
I brought it me nigh,
And I breathed a deep sigh,
As I turned it round and round.

Without beauty or breath,
Without knowledge in death,
Of any who passes it near.
Not a tooth could I trace,
Not a tongue in its place,
Nor a throat with its music to cheer.

No flush on that cheek,
'Tis both bare and bleak,
Without ear to hear my lay.
In its nostrils no breath,
But the stillness of death,
Its flesh is all wasted away !

Its eyes without light,
Without eyelids or sight,
Its footsteps to guide in the way.
The worms of the dust
Have made them a feast,
Scooping both of them clean away.

The brain that bore sway
Is all melted away,
Not a thought to it now belongs ;
　　Nor does it revolve
　　One single resolve
Of returning to right its wrongs.

　　Thy face gives no lore,
　　Who wert thou of yore,
If King or Duke thou hast stood.
　　Alexander the Great
　　Differs nothing in state
From his slave that died without food.

　　Grave-digger come near,
　　Say now in mine ear,
Whose skull in my hand I keep ;
　　That ask him I may,
　　While he lived, what his way,
Though never a word he'll speak.

　　Wer't a maid full of grace,
　　With a beautiful face,
And a soft glowing eye without flaw,—
　　Thy beauty a net,
　　That was skilfully set,
To capture each youth that thee saw ?

　　Thy charms are all gone,
　　That love to thee won,
And are now become a disgust.
　　Accurst be the tomb
　　That blighted thy bloom,
And turn'd thy fair form into dust.

A judge hast thou been,
Of sight clear and keen,
To discern the right from wrong ;
Who truth would not wrest,
But do what was just,
To all whether weak or strong ?

Or justice hast sold,
For an handful of gold,
To such as in place were high ;
And abandoned the poor,
To tyranny sure
ho could not thy favours buy ?

If thou didst do so,
And justice forego,
And crooked the straight didst make ;
As surely as death
Did take thee from earth,
Thou wast cast to the brimstone lake.

Or had'st thou great skill
Diseases to heal,—
All kinds of maladies sore ;
Proclaiming thy power,
As matchless to cure,
And snatch us from death's very door ?

Alas, that thy skill
Forsook thee when ill,
When assailed by thy malady sore ;
No plaster could ease,
Nor heal thy disease,
Or keep thee from death for an hour.

Did a captain thee own,
Who earned great renown—
A commander an army to lead ;
Subduing his foes,
Who up 'gainst him rose,
And strewing the field with dead ?

How left thee thy power,
And skill in that hour,
When met thee the host of the tomb ;
When yield thee thou must,
To the worms of the dust,
And submit to thy lowly doom ?

The worms on thee seize,
To do as they please,
E'en on thee each day to feast ;
The skull of thy head
Is a garrison made,
For the beetle to take his rest.

Some bore thy teeth
Inside of thy mouth,
While others are rending thine ear ;
And hoards of them try
To escape by thine eye,
To feed on thy cheek so blear.

Or a drunkard hast been,
In the tavern oft seen,
Carousing and drinking thy dram ;
And who sought not of bliss
For thyself than just this,
That thy brain in its fumes should swim ?

Or a man hast thou been,
Of a virtuous mien,
When you held your social feasts,
The lusts of thine heart
Were restrained on thy part,
What time you sat with thy guests ?

Wert a glutton as great,
As greedy of meat,
As dogs when devouring food ;
To satiate lust
With its cravings accurst,—
While making thy belly thy God ?

That belly is now
To which thou didst bow,
Quite full both of sand and earth ;
Thy teeth are at rest,
And thy tongue without taste,
Fast bound in the fetters of death.

A lord was he once,
In hand that does chance,
With acres both many and broad—
Who clothed the poor
That came to his door,
And from his rich stores them fed ?

Or remorseless wast thou,
In exacting thy due,
Oppressing thy men with rent ;
With severity sore,
Laying hands on their store,
Though poverty cried relent ?

Old men would not dare,
Who from age had no hair,
Themselves present in thy sight,
Without bonnet in hand
In thy presence to stand,
Though the frost their ears should blight.

Now thy slave may come near,
Nor do homage nor fear,
Despoiled thou'rt of state and store.
O praise be to death,
That under the earth,
Has restrained thy pride and power.

'Tis a Pastor perchance,
That faithfully once,
And earnestly plead in God's name,
Their steps to arrest,
Who travelled in haste
To perdition's destroying flame.

Or a stepmother thou—
Not regarding thy vow,
No love to the fold you had.
If the fleece you possesst,
Cared not for the rest,
Though foxes the flock should lead.

Most surely you had
The reward of your deed,
From the *Shepherd* when Him you met;
When summoned you were
To stand at His bar,
And be judged at His judgment seat.

Or is it a scull
Of dark projects was full,
And who with skill and with strength
   Did put them in force,
   Without fear or remorse,
He'd answer to God at length ?

   On slander wast bent,
   Without fear or restraint,
While taking thy lying way ;
   Full of poison thy tongue,
   Like a serpent did sting,
And hundreds did wound each day ?

   It is now at rest,
   'Neath death's strong arrest,
Never more to slander one ;
   Worms made it their prey,
   Till it wasted away,
To rot in its place in their turn.

   And if you lived so,
   Till death laid you low,
Not repenting thy sins so great ;
   Take rest in the grave,—
   All the Heaven thou'lt have—
Till arraigned at God's judgment seat.

   Like an ugly frog
   That crawls from a bog,
You'll ascend from the pit below,
   Christ Jesus to meet,
   At His judgment seat,
To sentence thee back to go.

For you'll be arraigned,
And as surely condemned,
To be driven for ever away ;
To consume in the fire,
Prepared in God's ire,
For the devil who led astray.

God shall harden your bones,
Hard as iron or stones,
And thy sinews as brazen thong.
He'll tighten thy flesh,
Like an anvil they thresh,
That fire can't consume tho' strong.

Or wert thou a head,
That truly knew God,
And pleased Him by doing the right ;
Though naked thou art,
Not knowing thy part,
Without tongue or nose or sight ?

Take courage ev'n now,
Rise surely shalt thou,
When thou'lt hear the trumpet blast.
Thy corruption thou'lt leave
Behind in the grave,
To loathsome worms of the dust.

God shall thee adorn
With beauty like morn,
As dawns it in rosy red.
He'll put light in those eyes,
And as stars in the skies
They'll shine as bright in thy head.

Thy tongue He'll untie,
To praise Him on high,
In glorious mansions above ;
He'll open thine ear,
Their songs there to hear
Who extol for ever His love.

When Christ comes again,
In glory to reign,
And to gather His Saints on high ;
Thou'lt hasten to meet
Thy Saviour great,
As swiftly as eagles can fly. ·

And when thou'lt arise,
He'll hail thee from skies,
To enjoy His friendship dear ;
And never to part
From the love of His heart,
Or Himself, in that glorious sphere.

Who hearest my lay,
Repent, nor delay
While health and reason do last
Ere death lay thee low,
And ne'er let thee go
To partake of the heavenly rest.

TURNBULL AND SPEARS, PRINTERS EDINBURGH.

www.ingramcontent.com/pod-product-compliance
Lightning Source LLC
Chambersburg PA
CBHW030553040726
47497CB00008B/2705